"What about  an affair?"
Xavier asked

Letty went still in... Her mind was try... proposing. "I'm not... you!"

"Why not? Who better to have an affair with than the man you once loved enough to marry?" As he caressed the warm nape of her neck, Letty relaxed.

"But I don't know all that much about you," she said, suddenly remembering the warning her friend Molly had given her.

"Sure you do. If you have any questions, you can always check my references," he said, caressing her mouth with his.

Molly's words came back. *There is no record of Xavier Augustine existing until ten years ago.* Letty wondered what Xavier would say if she asked for a list of people who'd known him for longer than ten years.

"Look," she said, panicking as she felt the familiar wild rush of longing, "I have to think."

"That's the old Letty talking," he murmured as his hands started their sensuous journey down her back. "The new Letty doesn't think her way through a decision. She *surrenders* to the moment . . . ."

Too Wild to Wed?

JAYNE ANN KRENTZ

MILLS & BOON LIMITED
ETON HOUSE, 18-24 PARADISE ROAD
RICHMOND, SURREY TW9 1SR

First published in Great Britain in 1991 by Mills & Boon Limited, Eton House, 18-24 Paradise Road, Richmond, Surrey TW9 1SR

© Jayne Ann Krentz 1991

ISBN 0 263 77558 5

21 – 9111

Made and printed in Great Britain

1

XAVIER AUGUSTINE WAS BACK in Tipton Cove.

Letty Conroy heard the arrogant purr of the hunter-green Jaguar and eagerly looked out her study window. It was nearly midnight and the storm that had been hovering offshore earlier that day had finally struck land an hour ago. Through a solid sheet of cold Oregon rain Letty watched the elegant car pull into her narrow drive. Her heart soared. Xavier was back a whole day early.

And he had come directly here to her, Letty realized, even though it was very late. Right here to her house. At midnight, no less. What would the neighbors think? she wondered with a soft, delighted chuckle.

She wanted to do more than chuckle. She wanted to laugh out loud. No, she wanted to sing. Xavier Augustine might look like a raffish, decidedly dangerous thug, but the truth was he had the manners of a saint.

Showing up here at her front door at this hour was completely out of character for him. Xavier, Letty had learned to her chagrin, was never the least bit improper. Since he had first started courting her three months ago, and *courting* was definitely the appropriate word, he had been the very soul of propriety. Indeed, he had been excruciatingly circumspect in every aspect of his wooing.

It could be rather depressing, not to say distinctly frustrating, to be romanced in such an old-fashioned manner. Letty had discovered to her astonishment during the past few months that she was apparently a woman of passion. She just wished she could find a way to set that passion free. She knew now that the only man who was capable of doing so was Xavier. But until now he had shown very little interest in the task.

The blunt truth was that Letty had never met a man so concerned with a woman's reputation, at least not in this century. Xavier's behavior had begun to seem uncomfortably close to that of some medieval lord bent on protecting his lady's honor at all costs.

It was true Tipton Cove was a very small academic town and Letty's position as an assistant professor of medieval studies at Tipton College was vulnerable to gossip. A certain level of deportment was expected of the faculty of the college. And, as she had reminded herself over and over again, it was wonderful in this day and age to meet a man who cared about protecting a woman from wagging tongues.

Nevertheless, she feared Xavier took his concern for her reputation a bit too far. After all, the man had dated her for nearly three months before asking her to marry him a week ago but he had yet to take her to bed.

Letty admitted to having had a few qualms concerning her beloved's sexual orientation at first. But her own woman's instincts reassured her. The hint of fire in Xavier's kisses and the glimpses of raw, glittering sensuality she had seen in his catlike green eyes when she had surprised him covertly studying her were unmistakable proof of his all-male eagerness.

No, the flames were there, all right, but for some inexplicable reason Xavier kept them carefully banked.

Lately she had begun to wonder if he suffered from some physical difficulty that he was too embarrassed to confess. She wanted to tell him she would understand and would love him regardless of his prowess in the bedroom, but she was too shy to bring up the subject for fear of insulting him.

It was all very complicated, Letty thought.

Out in the drive the door of the Jag closed with the soft, solid chunking sound made by very expensive, very classy car doors. Everything about Xavier Augustine was first-class and expensive—something else that had given Letty an occasional qualm in the midst of the magic of the past three months.

She was not used to going first-class on a college professor's salary.

Letty watched her fiancé stride quickly toward the old-fashioned porch that fronted her quaintly detailed Victorian-style house. Xavier seemed unconcerned with the rain pelting down on his thick dark hair. He had an expensive leather briefcase in one hand and a superbly tailored jacket slung over his arm. He wore European clothes—his shirt had been made in France, his shoes in Italy and his tie, which was unknotted and hung loose around his throat, came from England. The gold and steel chronometer on his muscled wrist had been precision engineered in Switzerland.

The man looked like a walking advertisement for the elegant, civilized life, but all the expensive accoutrements in the world could not conceal the very earthy, excitingly uncivilized, bluntly masculine aura he projected. At least not to Letty. She had been drawn to him from the first moment like a moth to the flame.

Xavier was a lean, tall, broad-shouldered man and he moved with the easy coordination of a hunting cat. He was thirty-eight years old, Letty knew, but there was no sign of softness about him. She doubted if there ever would be, regardless of his age or physical status. The hardness came from within and was a trait of the man himself. In the harsh yellow glare of the porch light she could see the rough planes and angles of his subtly fierce face. His eyes glittered in the shadows.

As Xavier approached, Letty felt a primeval thrill sweep through her—a very female sense of anticipation. She stood up quickly, leaving the last of the stack of exam papers she had been grading on the desk. She tightened the sash of her prim, high-necked, quilted robe as she hurried toward the door. Her thick fluffy slippers made no sound on the bare wood floor in the hall.

Xavier was here. At midnight, no less.

Letty caught a brief glimpse of herself in the hall mirror and winced. The problem with unexpected midnight callers was that you never had the chance to properly prepare for them. She thought about the dainty, frivolous lingerie she had bought for her trousseau this past week and sighed with regret. Everything was carefully packed in tissue and stashed in the bottom drawer of her dresser. There was no time to change into the beautiful peach-colored peignoir she had picked out with loving care last Saturday. Nor was there any time to apply some lipstick or take down her hair from the lopsided knot on top of her head.

The doorbell chimed impatiently. Letty pushed her glasses up higher on her nose and went through the clumsy, time-consuming ritual of unhooking the chain, unlocking the deadbolt and unlatching the new door lock, all of which Xavier had insisted she have installed two months ago. The man had a strong protective streak.

Letty at last got the door unsealed and opened it with a sense of exuberant excitement. She could always unpack the peach-colored peignoir, she told herself.

"*Xavier.*"

Then she got a good look at the man she loved and knew that he was not in any condition to sweep her off her feet and into bed tonight. Concern welled up, nudging aside the hopeful passion.

"Good heavens. I wasn't expecting you. You look absolutely exhausted. You must have had an awful drive in this storm." She touched the side of his face with her fingertips as she stood on tiptoe to brush her mouth a bit shyly against his.

His lips were hard and warm and she could smell the distinctly masculine scent—hints of his aftershave, leather from the car's upholstery and rain all in one.

"Sorry about the time, honey," he said. "I know I shouldn't have surprised you like this. I was going to wait until morning. But when I landed in Portland a couple of hours ago I just got into the car and kept driving toward the coast. I considered waking up somebody down at the motel, but I decided I'd come over here instead." His teeth gleamed briefly in his familiar, fleeting smile. He was very sure of his welcome. "Do you mind?"

"Oh, no, not in the least." Letty blushed happily, not caring that her feelings for him were blatantly obvious. She reached out hastily and took the briefcase from him. "Here, let me take that." She staggered backward a step under the unexpected weight of the leather case and realized she needed both hands to lift it.

He frowned. "Are you sure you can handle that?"

"Of course. My own weighs almost as much. Come on in, Xavier, and don't worry about the time. I mean, we are engaged, after all, aren't we? It's freezing out there. And you're soaking wet."

"Thanks. It's really coming down." He ran his fingers through his dark hair, shaking off water droplets onto the rug. Then he blocked a huge yawn with the back of his hand. "Just set that down anywhere. I'll go back out and get my suitcase in a few minutes. Hell, I'm really beat. I thought Waverly would never sign those papers. Took me all day to talk him into it."

"But your business went well?"

"No major problems." He yawned again and rubbed the back of his neck. "Unless you count jet lag."

"Why don't you go on into the parlor and sit down. I'll make you a nice cup of tea."

"I'd rather have a shot of brandy."

"Brandy. Oh, yes. Certainly. Brandy." Letty thought fast. "I've got some, I think. I'll get it right away. You can put your jacket in the hall closet."

"Right. Thanks."

Anxious to please him so that he would be more inclined to stay, Letty hauled the briefcase halfway down the hall, dropped it on the floor with a thud and rushed into the kitchen.

Please let there be some brandy left in the cupboard, she prayed silently. *And please let it be a decent label.*

"Did you get your portion of the invitation list made up?" Xavier called out casually from the parlor.

"Yes. The invitations will go out next week. Everyone on the faculty is included, just like you said. And the library staff. And the trustees."

"I brought my list with me. You can add the names to yours."

"Is it very long?" Letty asked, trying to keep the uneasiness out of her voice. She opened a cupboard and discovered to her relief that she did, indeed, have some brandy left. Unfortunately it was an unprepossessing label that she had purchased primarily to use in cooking. Xavier was bound to notice. He was very aware of such things. He would never buy cheap brandy, not even for cooking.

"No. Only about fifty people or so. Business acquaintances for the most part. I don't have any family to invite, as I told you."

Fifty? Letty rolled her eyes heavenward and stifled a groan as she reflected on the added effort of addressing fifty more wedding invitations. Xavier had taken three months to ask her to marry him but once he'd popped the question and gotten Letty's immediate answer, he'd moved forward with ruthless efficiency to set events in motion.

Before he'd left on this latest business trip, he'd given her a long list of tasks to do in preparation for the wedding, which he had decreed would be at the end of the month.

When she'd asked why the rush, he'd told her he liked the idea of a June wedding. It was traditional, he'd explained with an air of authority that had made her smile. She was given to understand Xavier Augustine wanted a formal affair with all the trappings. First class, all the way.

Letty had been working like a demon for the past couple of weeks what with having to grade end-of-term papers and exams while trying to plan the full-scale wedding production Xavier had insisted upon having. She would not have accomplished nearly as much as she had in the short span of time if not for the help of her friend, Molly Sweet.

"Guess what?" Letty called brightly, as she hurried out of the kitchen with the two glasses and the bottle of brandy. "I went shopping for the dress with Molly and we found the most gorgeous gown. I can't wait for you to see me in it."

"I'm looking forward to it," Xavier said. He sounded indulgent.

"It's really beautiful. Sort of old-fashioned looking with a square neckline and loads of white lace and little pearls around the hem and yards and yards of petticoats and skirts and—ouch." Letty broke off abruptly as her toe struck the massive briefcase in the hall. She sucked in her breath and squeezed her eyes shut for a few seconds. "Damn."

"You okay?" Xavier asked from the parlor.

"I'm fine. Just fine. No problem, really." Letty gritted her teeth and stood on one foot while she waited for the pain to subside in the other. At least she had not spilled the brandy, she noticed. A small miracle under the circumstances. "Be right there."

"I think I'll build a fire. All right with you?"

"Yes, please go ahead. Sounds lovely." Letty glowered at the briefcase as she went past. Then she forgot about her sore toe as it dawned on her that it was looking more and more as if Xavier meant to spend the entire night here.

Her rising sense of euphoria plummeted briefly when she reminded herself he would probably insist upon sleeping on the sofa. But just maybe, it she got enough brandy into him, he could be persuaded to head for the bedroom.

Oh, Lord. After all these months of anticipation and frustrated desire and the deepest sense of longing she had ever known, maybe *tonight* would be the night.

Letty rounded the corner into what had once been the front parlor of the old Victorian house and saw that Xavier was down on one knee setting a match to a pile of kindling on the hearth. He had removed his tie. His white shirt was open at the throat and the sleeves were rolled up on his sinewy forearms. He glanced up as she entered the room and she realized again how drawn and tired he looked.

"Just what I need," Xavier remarked, his eyes moving to the brandy. He finished lighting the fire and got to his feet.

He took the bottle of brandy and one of the glasses from her hand. Letty held her breath as he briefly examined the label. But he made no comment as he filled both glasses.

"What a hell of a day." He swallowed half the contents of the glass and smiled wearily at her, green eyes glinting in the light of the rising flames. He brushed his knuckles affectionately along her cheek. "You look good, honey. I missed you."

"I'm glad. I missed you, too." Letty wanted to catch hold of his hand and keep his knuckles pressed against her skin. She wondered why the bubble of happiness on which she was standing did not simply leave the ground entirely and carry her up to the ceiling.

All the hard work of the past week was suddenly totally unimportant. In another three and a half weeks she would be married to this man and it would all be worth it. She raised the brandy glass to her lips and firelight sparkled on the large emerald in her beautiful engagement ring.

"I got a couple of things accomplished beside closing the Waverly deal," Xavier said matter-of-factly, as he walked across the room and sat down on the chintz sofa. "Picked up the cruise tickets."

"Did you really? How exciting. Did you bring them with you?" The one thing Xavier had insisted on handling personally was booking the honeymoon cruise. Letty knew he planned to take her first-class and she was quite dazzled by the prospect. She had never been on a luxury cruise.

Xavier smiled slightly at her obvious enthusiasm. "The tickets are in my briefcase. Along with a brochure describing the ports of call." He sprawled on the sofa and unbuttoned another shirt button. Firelight revealed the shadows beneath his eyes and the hollows below his high cheekbones.

"I'll go and get your briefcase," Letty said readily. She set down her brandy glass and hurried toward the hallway. "I can't wait to see the brochure."

Out in the hall she found the massive leather briefcase, seized it with both hands and dragged it back into the parlor.

"You're such a little thing," Xavier observed. "Better let me handle that." He went to pick up the briefcase and opened it, pulling out a colorful brochure. "Here you go. What do you think? Does it look like the perfect honeymoon trip?"

Letty took the brochure and opened it eagerly. Brilliant photographs of tropical islands, a gleaming white ship and a seemingly endless array of exotic shipboard food was spread before her. "Xavier, it looks fabulous. I can see I'm going to have to do some more shopping, though. I don't have the right kind of clothes for a trip like this."

"Get whatever you need. And don't worry about the cost. I'll pick up the tab." Xavier downed the rest of his brandy and leaned into the corner of the sofa, resting his head on the high cushioned back. He massaged the bridge of his nose, gazed into the flames and stifled another yawn with the back of his hand.

"No, you will not pick up the tab, thank you very much." Letty turned another page in the brochure and scanned an array of scenes that showed happy couples drifting about on the ship's dance floor. "I have a perfectly good career, remember? Tipton College may not pay the best faculty salaries in the state, but I can certainly afford my own clothes."

"I want you to have the right things for the trip." Xavier frowned slightly and poured himself a little more brandy. "We'll be traveling first-class and I want you to feel—" he paused "—comfortable among the other passengers. Clothes have a lot to do with how others treat you—how much they respect you."

"I suppose so." Letty bit her lip and risked a quick glance at Xavier. He was still studying the dancing flames, his dark lashes half-closed as he lounged wearily on the sofa. He had one elegantly shod foot up on the coffee table and he looked as if he was about to fall asleep.

This was probably not the best time to tell him she was not particularly concerned with how expensively dressed she was on the cruise, Letty decided judiciously.

The issue of Xavier's insistence on always doing things first-class would have bothered her more if she had not sensed intuitively that he did not actually judge others by how well they dressed or how much money they made. He certainly had not judged her by her clothes or her income, which was nowhere near his.

Nor did Xavier treat others differently according to their financial status. Money or the lack of it was obviously not the issue for him when it came to dealing with people.

But Xavier liked having the best for himself; he insisted on doing things in what he called the right way, the proper way.

Letty was beginning to think there was something about the outward trappings of what he termed *class*, that were too important to Xavier Augustine. At times it was almost as if he had something to prove. And yet there was so much sheer arrogant strength in him, she reminded herself. It was one of the many aspects of the man that had initially attracted her. Surely he had nothing to prove to anyone.

Xavier Augustine was as solid as a rock in all the ways that counted. Once he made a commitment, you knew he would stand by it come hell or high water. That sense of reassuring strength was something Letty had never found in any other man, something she had been waiting all of her life to find.

Now, for the first time, she wondered if it was possible for a man to be *too* strong, too self-controlled, too intent on running his own private world. As she watched Xavier doze in front of the fire she finally acknowledged that part of her was definitely getting worried about the relationship in which she found herself.

She did not know all that much about Xavier Augustine. In fact, all she really knew was what everyone else in Tipton Cove knew. He was a quietly but brilliantly successful entrepreneur, an independent consultant and owner of his own firm, a company called Augustine Consulting. A few months ago he had been invited by the chairman of Tipton College's newly established School of Business Administration to give a series of guest lectures.

The lectures had been popular beyond the chairman's fondest dreams. They had been riveting. Several members of the faculty outside the School of Business Administration, such as Letty Conroy from the history department, had heard about them and dropped into the lecture hall on Wednesday afternoons to see what all the excitement was about. Letty had not been disappointed, although she was the first to admit the subject of business held little innate interest for her.

Tipton College had not been disappointed, either. In addition to a lively series of lectures, Xavier had endeared himself forever to the small private college by personally endowing a faculty chair in the School of Business Administration. It was, of course, to be called the Xavier Augustine Chair in Business Administration. Certain delighted trustees were privately calling it the Saint Augustine Chair.

Letty had been introduced to Xavier at a faculty tea. She had been shy initially, acutely conscious of Xavier's effect on her senses. It had taken her a while to realize that what she was experiencing for the first time at the age of twenty-nine was a compelling physical and emotional attraction to a man. The effect was almost lethal to her inexperienced senses. She'd had an occasional crush in the past but nothing like this.

She had struggled valiantly to deal with the unfamiliar overwhelming sensations and had tried to conceal her rioting reactions behind a ladylike facade. Then

Xavier had smiled at her in such a way she'd instinctively sensed the attraction was mutual.

From that point on Letty knew she had not stood a chance. Xavier had pursued her with an archaic correctness and an attention to propriety that would have graced the most chivalrous knight of old, but he had definitely *pursued* her. There had been no doubt of that.

Looking back on the past three months, Letty decided it was just as well she had been attracted to her modern knight from the start because she was not at all certain she could have escaped him.

Now she was engaged to marry him. She gazed down at the beautifully designed gold and emerald ring she wore. It had, of course, been purchased from a jeweler who dealt only in the finest gems. Xavier had selected the ring himself. In the glow of the firelight the elegant stone reflected the same fire Letty occasionally saw in his eyes.

This marriage would work, she told herself fiercely. There were some unknowns in the equation, but surely she could trust her instincts. She loved this man, even if she did not know a great deal about him. Everyone approved of Xavier, from the college president right down to the secretaries in Admissions. She was not making a terrible mistake, Letty told herself. She was seizing the opportunity of a lifetime. Everyone said so.

"Xavier," Letty said tentatively, "I was just wondering if you planned to, well, you know, stay here tonight? I mean, it's perfectly all right with me. Goodness knows there's plenty of room and I wouldn't mind in the least. In fact, I . . ."

Letty's voice trailed off into thin air as she looked up from the colorful brochure and realized the love of her life had fallen asleep on her sofa. Disappointment gripped her for a moment. And then a rueful amusement made her smile to herself. There was no way she would ever be able to get him into her bed tonight. And she really did hate to wake him. He looked so exhausted.

She got to her feet and went to fetch a blanket from the hall closet. Her initial disappointment faded a little as she realized that even though he was not actually in her bed, Xavier was going to spend the night right here in her cozy little house. Definitely a step in the right direction. It was better than having him go back to the Seaside Motel the way he had all the other nights of their courtship.

Tenderly Letty removed the expensive Italian shoes and arranged Xavier's legs on the sofa. It was not easy. Everything about Xavier was strong, smoothly muscled and surprisingly heavy.

Eventually she managed to get him looking halfway comfortable. He mumbled something once as she bent over him to adjust the blanket.

"What did you say?" she whispered.

He opened one glittering green eye and regarded her with a sleepy, blatantly sexy expression. His mouth quirked. Then he lifted his hand and wrapped it around the nape of her neck. His fingers were warm and strong and very sure.

"I said, you're sweet," he muttered, dragging her down so that he could kiss her. His mouth moved lazily, lingeringly, on hers. His tongue slid briefly into her warmth. "You even taste sweet. Almost too good to be true. But you are, aren't you?"

"Well, I certainly hope I'm not *that* good." She laughed at him with her eyes. "It sounds dull."

He shook his head slowly and closed his eyes again. "Not dull. Suitable. Classy. Just what I wanted. You're exactly the way you're supposed to be—a real lady." He turned his head into the cushion and exhaled deeply. "I've got the proof," he concluded in a soft, indistinct mumble.

"Xavier?" Letty straightened and stared down at him uncertainly. "What proof? What do you mean by that?"

But Xavier was sound asleep. Letty did not have the heart to shake him awake and demand an explanation. Perhaps he'd been half caught up in a dream.

She took a step backward and the back of her leg collided with the heavy briefcase. The leather case toppled over, spilling some of its contents onto the rug.

Letty hurriedly bent down to collect the various papers and manila envelopes that had fallen out. She glanced automatically at the documents as she started to stuff them back into the briefcase.

The first envelope bore the name of a small Oregon bank. The second had Waverly written on it in Xavier's bold scrawl and the third, a legal-sized envelope, had her first name jotted on it in pencil in the upper right-hand corner. *Letty.*

Xavier's writing again. Something he'd meant to give her, Letty decided. Perhaps more information on the cruise trip he had planned.

Letty stared at the envelope and then turned it slowly in her hands to read the return address. Her insides went cold as she realized she was looking at the name of a Portland-based firm of private investigators. Hawkbridge Investigations.

You're exactly the way you're supposed to be. I've got the proof.

Letty could not believe her eyes. She held the envelope as if it were about to explode in her hands. Surely Xavier had not had her investigated. He was smart and savvy and as hard as nails in some ways, but surely he would not have chosen a bride based on the recommendation of a private detective agency. Perhaps it was all a mistake. Perhaps her name jotted on the outside of the envelope had nothing to do with the contents.

Letty moved to the chair in front of the fire and sat huddled there for a long while, the envelope in front of her. The longer she stared at it, the more certain she was that she had to find out what was inside. She was dealing with her future here.

She looked across at the sofa and saw that Xavier was deeply asleep. Then she lowered her eyes once more to the ominous envelope. Slowly she opened it and pulled out two sheets of paper. The first was a short, handwritten note scrawled boldly on Hawkbridge Investigations letterhead:

Here's the final report, Xav. I ran the check myself, as I said I would and it was done with complete discretion. There were no surprises, as you will see when you read it.

Ms. Conroy has obviously spent the past twenty-nine years just sitting around waiting for you to show up. Take some advice and marry her fast before someone else gets his hands on her. Your bride-to-be is exactly what you've been looking for, a real lady.

Don't forget to invite me to the wedding,

Hawk

With dawning horror Letty unfolded the second sheet

of paper and read the report the investigation agency had compiled for Xavier.

When she was finished, she wept.

When the tears were dried she sat for a long while staring into the flames. And then she made her decision.

2

He was drowning in a white sea.

Xavier came awake with a start and slashed at the billowing creamy white satin that was threatening to suffocate him. He sucked in his breath and got a mouthful of pearl-studded lace, which he promptly spit out.

"What the hell?" He was buried beneath waves of white petticoat netting, trapped by yards of heavy, gleaming white fabric that covered him from head to foot.

He jackknifed to a sitting position on the sofa and fought free of the frothy white fog, finally surfacing beneath the folds of a wedding veil to see Letty on the other side of the room.

She was wearing a pair of jeans that snugly fitted her sweetly shaped derriere. Xavier had an excellent view of that derriere, even through the veil, because Letty was bent over at the waist, thrusting something red and frilly into an open suitcase.

Slowly he lifted the delicate netting away from his face. His first thought was that he had fallen asleep like a damn fool instead of making love to Letty last night as he had intended.

He had spent the whole of the long night drive from Portland thinking about taking Letty to bed. The time had finally arrived, he had told himself with a great deal of satisfaction. He had all the reports, the engagement was official and Letty was waiting to fall into the palm of his hand like a sweet, ripe plum. He planned to catch her very gently.

But the long, frustrating business trip to conclude the Waverly deal followed by the drive to the coast had taken more out of him than he had realized. Apparently he'd collapsed on the sofa after only a couple of glasses of Letty's lamentable California brandy. Xavier made a mental note to buy her a bottle of the good French stuff.

He stared for a moment at the cold ashes on the hearth and then at the yards of white satin that surrounded him and wondered if he was still dreaming. Something was definitely wrong but he could not imagine what it could be. Everything was supposed to be under control.

"Do you like the wedding gown, Xavier?" Letty asked in a strangely brittle voice. She did not turn around. "I certainly hope so, because it goes straight back to the store today. This is the only opportunity you'll ever have to see it."

"Good morning to you, too." Xavier pushed aside another wave of white satin and wondered what had gone awry in his neatly constructed world.

"Don't you dare call this a good morning." Letty straightened and spun around to glare at him through her little tortoiseshell glasses. "This is the worst morning of my life. The only thing good about it is that I have at last discovered the truth about my knight in shining armor. He's a no-good, rotten, scheming, conniving untrusting sonofa—"

"That's enough." Xavier held up a hand to silence her. "Not first thing in the morning, if you don't mind. I need a cup of coffee before I can deal with this. And after the cup of coffee, I'd like an explanation. A rational, straightforward, logical explanation, not a lot of feminine screeching."

"If you don't like the sound of my *screeching*," Letty shrieked, "you can take your first-class cruise tickets and your first-class shoes, and my beautiful, first-class wedding gown and get into your first-class car and get out of my life. The sooner, the better, as far as I'm concerned."

Xavier experienced a twinge of genuine concern. He wondered if Letty was ill. He'd heard strange things about the effects of PMS. He also recalled hearing about something called bridal jitters. "Are you feeling all right, honey?"

"No, I am not feeling all right," she yelled furiously. Her small hands clenched into fists around a lacy little black bra. "I am feeling damned mad. And hurt. And I am totally disgusted with you, Xavier Augustine. I thought you were the love of my life but you're really an arrogant, cynical, self-centered clod. You don't love me. You never did love me."

"Letty," he said, wondering if she wore that little scrap of black lace regularly and if so what she looked like in it, "you're not making any sense."

"Who the hell do you think you are to have me investigated? What right did you have to check out my past to see if I was good enough to be your wife? How could you do that, Xavier Augustine? How could you do such a horrid, untrusting thing to me? I thought you *loved* me."

Xavier went very still as he finally began to realize what had happened. She must have found the letter from Hawkbridge Investigations. His gaze flicked to the briefcase. It yawned open revealing a myriad of envelopes, documents and papers. He did not see the incriminating envelope.

"I think you had better calm down and explain why you're so upset," Xavier said, opting for an air of calm authority.

"Why I'm upset? *Upset?*" She stared at him as if he'd lost his senses. "I'm not upset, I'm enraged. Outraged. Furious. Insulted to the core. Madder than hell. I'd like to stake you out over the nearest anthill and pour honey on you."

"Why?"

"Because I've just discovered you deliberately checked out my past before you did me the great honor of asking me to marry you. You had to make certain I was classy enough for you, didn't you? You had to see if I was good enough to go with your expensive car and your fancy wine and your hand-tailored suits."

He sighed. "So you did find that letter. I never meant for you to see it, Letty. I knew it might upset you."

"I told you, I'm a hell of a lot more than a trifle upset. What right did you have to that? I wasn't applying for the post of Queen of England, you know. If you wanted to find out about my sordid past, all you had to do was ask me. I would have told you everything. But, oh, no, you didn't trust me enough to just ask, did you? You had to run a full-scale investigation. How much did that fancy outfit charge you, anyway?"

Xavier smiled faintly and rubbed the back of his neck. "Your past is anything but sordid, honey," he pointed out gently. He ignored her question about the price of the investigation. Hawkbridge Investigations charged an arm and a leg for its services but it had been worth every penny as far as Xavier was concerned.

Hawk ran a top-notch, utterly reliable outfit. "There was nothing in the report to be embarrassed about."

"Oh, God, I know only too well there was nothing exciting or sordid to report on me. You don't have to remind me of what a dull life I've led until now." Letty dropped the black lace bra and stalked over to the table where a familiar-looking envelope lay. She shook out the report Xavier had commissioned on her. "Look at this. Just look at it."

Xavier glanced at the few brief lines on the page—evidence of a pristine past. He knew everything on that sheet by heart. His future wife was twenty-nine years old and well on her way to becoming an old maid.

She had grown up in a small town in eastern Washington, the unexpected and rather late-in-life child of a highly respected local judge and the daughter of one of the county's oldest, most established families.

Letty's parents, who had long since given up on the possibility of having children, had been thrilled with and quite overprotective of their little girl right from the start. They had also been unusually strict with her, at least by modern standards of child rearing. As staunch pillars of the local community, the judge and his wife had impressed upon their one and only child the supreme importance of not doing anything to disgrace them or herself.

In spite of her carefully supervised upbringing, or perhaps because of it, Letty had been a happy, well-loved child who had displayed her intellectual abilities early on and been encouraged to develop them. She had been a model student all the way through high school and college, never once getting into any kind of mischief. She had rarely even dated.

Her history studies had been her chief interest in life and she had concentrated on them to the exclusion of almost everything else. She had graduated with honors in history and gone on to complete a Ph.D in Medieval studies at a small, private, very distinguished college back east. She had returned to the Pacific Northwest to join the faculty of Tipton College the year she had completed her studies.

A copy of Letty's doctoral dissertation, a lengthy treatise entitled *An Examination of the Status of Women in the Medieval World*, had been included along with the preliminary report from the investigation. Xavier had read every word. He had also read several of the papers and articles she'd had published in obscure academic history journals since graduating.

Her parents had been killed in the crash of a small plane piloted by Letty's father four years ago. Since their death Letty had continued to lead a quiet, decorous existence that consisted of a busy round of study, teaching, research and faculty teas.

In addition, there were occasional trips to England during summer vacations where she toured castles and buried herself for days on end in such places as the Bodleian Library and the British Museum.

Until Xavier had arrived on the scene, Letty's relationship with men had been limited to the occasional quiet date with a fellow member of the history department. During the past year a certain Dr. Sheldon Peabody, an associate professor also specializing in medieval history, had escorted Letty to a handful of chamber music performances and a production of *Hamlet*. Letty had been home shortly after midnight on each occasion and Peabody had hung around just long enough for a cup of tea before taking his leave.

Xavier had made it a point to meet Dr. Sheldon Peabody and had not been particularly worried by the competition.

All in all, Xavier had concluded early on, Letty Conroy was an eminently suitable wife for him. There was an air of class about her. *Real* class. The kind that could not be faked or bought or learned—the kind *he* had worked so hard to cultivate.

Letty was not stunningly beautiful, but he had learned long ago not to let himself be blinded by a woman's superficial attractions. In any event, her lively features held a piquant charm and intelligence that appealed to him on a deep, fundamental level.

She had huge hazel eyes, a tip-tilted nose and a soft, vulnerable mouth that responded beautifully to Xavier's kisses. She was slender and feminine with high, round, pert little breasts. Her hair, which she almost always wore in a classic knot at the nape of her neck, was a thick, lustrous chestnut color. Last night it had glowed with the reflected light of the fire. As he had drifted off to sleep, Xavier had imagined flames burning in that thick, sleek hair.

And she had the most delightful way of deferring to his wishes, Xavier reminded himself a bit smugly. She was always terribly anxious to please him.

She also had excellent manners, stimulating conversation, a sweet temperament and she was head-over-heels in love with Xavier Augustine. Most important of all, she was an honorable, old-fashioned sort of woman who would take such things as wedding vows very seriously.

The perfect wife—an eminently suitable wife. Exactly the sort of wife he wanted, Xavier thought with satisfaction and not for the first time. All he had to do now was smooth her ruffled feathers. Husbands had to do that sort of thing occasionally. He might as well get in some practice.

The truth was, he did not really mind this unexpected display of temper now that he was past the first shock of surprise. Temper indicated passion and he definitely wanted passion in his wife. He was a man of strong, sensual appetites himself and he could not imagine a worse fate than being married to a woman who did not respond to him physically.

"I was very pleased with that report," Xavier said carefully, searching for a way to defuse Letty's volatile mood. "It confirmed everything I already knew or suspected. You are exactly what you claimed to be."

"Well, you aren't what you claimed to be at all, Xavier Augustine. You're a fraud. Do you hear me? A complete fraud."

Xavier felt as if he'd been kicked in the stomach. For an instant, genuine panic set in. There was no way she could know the truth, he told himself desperately. No way at all. He had buried it long ago.

He found his breath with an effort and stood up abruptly to cover his startled response. "What are you talking about, Letty?"

"You let me think you were in love with me," Letty wailed. "I thought you trusted me. I thought you cared for me."

The sick feeling was washed away by a wave of relief. She did not know anything, after all. Xavier started toward the kitchen. "I do care for you. Very much. And I trust you, sweetheart." *I trust you completely now that I've seen that report*, he added silently. He smiled down at Letty and ducked his head to drop a quick kiss on her forehead as he went past.

She stepped back hurriedly but not in time to avoid the light, possessive touch of his mouth. Her eyes narrowed behind the lenses of her glasses as she glowered up at him. "If you trust me so much, why did you have that background check run on me?"

"Routine, honey. Just routine." He walked into the kitchen and started opening cupboard doors.

"Routine? You expect me to believe that?" She hurried down the hall after him and came to a halt in the kitchen doorway, her expression fierce. "I've got news for you, Xavier, it is definitely not routine to hire professional investigators to run checks on future spouses."

"It's not as rare as you think, Letty," he said quietly. "Not for a man in my position." He opened another door and found a package of coffee. "Ah, here we go. I'll be in better shape to defend myself after I've gotten some caffeine into my system. Are you always this feisty in the mornings?" He went across the room to where the drip coffee machine sat perched on a tiled counter.

"Don't you dare try to make a joke out of this." She stalked into the kitchen and snatched the package of coffee out of his unresisting hand. "I have been badly hurt and humiliated and I will not have you making fun of me on top of everything else."

"I'm not making fun of you, sweetheart." He leaned back against the counter and watched in amusement as she opened the package of coffee and measured some into the machine. This was his Letty, he thought with satisfaction, so very feminine in her ways that she was even making him coffee while she raged at him. It was touching. "And I assure you I never meant for you to be hurt or humiliated. That was the last thing on my mind."

"Is that right?" She shoved the glass pot under the faucet, filled it with water and dumped the water into the coffee machine. Then she stabbed the switch. "What was the first thing in your mind? Making certain I wasn't some floozy? Some gold digger who was going to try to take you to the cleaners? Give me a break, Xavier. I've got a perfectly good career of my own and I love it. I don't need your money and you ought to damn well know it."

"I never thought you were after my money," he said honestly.

"Then why the investigation? Did you think I'd murdered my last three husbands and buried them in the backyard or something?"

"No."

"What were you looking for, then?" she demanded, her voice rising another notch.

This was going to be a little difficult to explain, especially in her present mood. Xavier chose his words thoughtfully. "I did not go looking for anything in particular, Letty. I told you, it was just a routine background check."

She nodded with savage conviction. "Just a routine check to make certain I was worthy of being married to the great Saint Augustine. You wanted to make certain I was as first-class as everything else you own, didn't you? You had to make sure there were no embarrassing scandals in my past."

"Now, Letty..."

"No awkward little brushes with the law. No ex-husbands or alcoholic fathers or brothers lurking in the woodwork who happen to be compulsive gamblers. No family history of insanity or criminal connections.

That's what you wanted to check out, wasn't it? You wanted to see if I was really suitable wife material."

"Don't twist this all up into little knots you won't be able to unravel, Letty."

"Damn you, the least you owe me now is the truth. Admit you checked up on me because you had the un-mitigated gall to want to be certain I was good enough to be your wife."

"You're overreacting." Xavier was beginning to grow irritated now. "In this day and age when people marry strangers instead of the girl next door, it pays to be a little cautious." He'd learned that lesson the hard way, he reflected bitterly.

"Then you must think I'm a real idiot, because I didn't hire anyone to do a background check on you," she shot back. "Why on earth would you want to marry an id-iot? It's probably hereditary and you told me you want children."

"The coffee's finished."

She looked at the full pot in outraged horror. "Talk about idiocy. What on earth am I doing making coffee for you like a good little wife? I must be out of my mind." She yanked the pot out from under the filter basket and dumped the freshly brewed coffee down the sink.

Xavier winced. "That wasn't really necessary."

"Oh, yes it was," she stated, slamming the pot down onto the kitchen counter. "I am no longer going to ca-ter to you, Xavier Augustine. Our engagement was ended the minute I found that letter from the investi-gators. I need to start somewhere and this is as good a point as any."

He eyed her expression with misgivings. "What, ex-actly are you going to start?"

"Living a more exciting life," she announced. "Do you know what the worst thing was about that damn report the investigators filed on me?"

"Honey, there was nothing bad in that report."

"That was the worst thing about it," she stormed. "I looked at that report last night and realized that my entire life had been summarized in less than a single page. There wasn't one single, thrilling, scandalous item to put down. No torrid relationships, no danger-ous adventures, no unsavory incidents. The long and the short of it is, my life has been a dead bore to date."

"Damn it, there is nothing wrong in being a dead bore." Xavier closed his mouth abruptly but it was too late. The words had already been spoken and hung in the air like grenades waiting to explode.

"My God, that's the bottom line, isn't it?" Letty's eyes filled with horror. "You wanted to marry me precisely because I am a dead bore."

"I did not mean that the way it sounded and you know it," Xavier said through set teeth. "What I meant to say was that there is nothing wrong in having lived a blameless life. You should be proud of yourself."

"Well, I'm not. I'm furious when I think of what a little goody two-shoes I've been. And to be married for that reason is the final straw." Letty lifted her chin in proud defiance. "From now on, Xavier, I shall dedicate myself to only one goal and that goal will be to live a life-style that will absolutely, positively guarantee to make me totally unsuitable to be your wife."

She stomped back past him out of the kitchen, red flags of anger flying in her cheeks, her slender frame stiff with tension.

"I can't believe I'm hearing this." Xavier swung around and went after her. "Letty, you're behaving like a child. When you've had a chance to calm down, you'll realize you're completely overreacting."

"I'll overreact if that's what I feel like doing." She was back at the suitcase, tossing more frilly underwear inside. "From now on I will do whatever I feel like doing. No more Ms. Nice, Proper, Boring Dr. Conroy. Henceforth, I am a new woman and the last thing anyone will ever say about me in the future is that I'm untainted, unsullied or boring. I'm going to go for the gusto."

He scowled at the suitcase. "Are you planning to go somewhere in particular for this gusto?"

"Yes."

He drew a breath, telling himself to be patient. "Where?"

"None of your business, really. But since you ask and since I have no objection to telling you, I'll answer the question." Letty folded a tiny pair of red lace panties and placed them on top of what appeared to be a filmy peach-colored peignoir. "I am going to spend the next few days boning up on the pleasures of life in the fast lane."

Xavier stared at her. "What the hell are you talking about now?"

She straightened abruptly. "I am going to accept a long-standing invitation to attend the quarterly convention of what I understand to be a lively, fun-loving group of amateur historians called The Order of Medieval Revelers."

Xavier folded his arms across his chest and stood, legs braced, glaring at her. "And just who the hell issued this long-standing invitation?"

"Dr. Sheldon Peabody."

"*Peabody?* That pompous ass in the history department?"

"I believe you've met him at one or two of the faculty teas," Letty said in lofty tones. "He figures in the investigator's report as one of my 'occasional, insignificant relationships with members of the opposite sex.' I think that was how it was phrased. Such a delicate way of saying I have a boring love life."

"Stop calling your life boring," Xavier ordered.

"Any life that can be summed up in one page is boring. And while we're on the subject, I would like to take this opportunity to point out that my dull love life didn't get any more exciting after you came on the scene."

It took him a few seconds to realize the nature of the accusation she was hurling in his face. Xavier's jaw dropped. Then his teeth snapped together. "Now hold on one blasted minute here. Are you saying you're mad because I didn't take you to bed?"

"Not mad, just bored."

He lost his temper at that point and reached for her. "You know something, lady? You've got one hell of a lot of nerve."

"Don't touch me." Letty stepped back quickly but not quickly enough. Xavier's fingers closed around her shoulders and he hauled her up against his chest. Her wide, startled eyes were only inches away from his own furious gaze.

"Bored, were you?" he gritted. "After all I went through to behave like a gentleman? After all those nights I went back to the motel room alone and stood under a cold shower? And you have the nerve to tell me you were bored?"

She bit her lip. "Well, maybe bored isn't quite the right word."

"No, it is definitely not the right word."

She got a grip on herself and defiance blazed in her eyes once more. "Try frustrated. Or confused. Or worried."

"Worried about what, for crying out loud?"

She made a little sound to clear her throat and her eyes flickered uneasily. Her cheeks blushed a bright pink as she lowered her gaze to his chest. "I did wonder if perhaps you had some sort of, uh, masculine problem, if you know what I mean."

Xavier was so outraged he could barely think coherently. "A problem? Hell and damnation, woman. You better believe you won't have to worry much longer about any problem I might have in that department."

"Now, Xavier, there's no need to feel offended. Lots of men have problems of that sort," she said soothingly. "I've read all about them. I understand most of them can be quite easily remedied with modern medical technology. There are even little devices you can use to sort of pump yourself up, I hear—"

"*Not another word out of you*," he roared. "It will give me real pleasure to demonstrate that all the basic equipment I possess is in full working order. Trust me, by the time I've finished proving I don't have any problem in bed, you won't have any lingering questions left on the subject. You'll be lucky to be able to walk."

"Promises, promises," she taunted. "And stop yelling at me. You don't have any right to yell. Or to make threats. It was perfectly reasonable of me to question your sexual prowess under the circumstances. After all, I had no way of knowing you were simply biding your

time until you had the final report on my background."

"Damn it, Letty."

"Why did you wait? Weren't you attracted enough to
me to want to go to bed with me? Did it take that stupid report to make the thought of making love to me
bearable?"

"That's enough, Letty. You're carrying this whole
thing too far."

"It was your own future comfort you were really
thinking about, wasn't it? You'll be living full-time in
Tipton Cove now that you're moving your business
headquarters here. You'll be giving more guest lectures
at the college. You'll be socializing with all sorts of high-
profile, conservative, respectable people. I can see
where it would have been embarrassing to have had a
brief fling with one of the junior members of the history department. What if she made things a trifle awkward after you finally found a really *suitable* wife?"

"Letty, I'm warning you . . ."

"Admit it, Xavier. Admit you couldn't be bothered
to seduce me until you were sure I was good enough for
you. You know something? I think that is the final insult."

"That does it. You're beyond reason at the moment.
I'm getting out of here while you cool down." Xavier
released her before he lost any more of his normally
ironclad self-control. He strode across the room and put
on his shoes. Then he snatched the offending letter from
the investigation firm off the end table, shoved it into
the briefcase and latched the buckles.

Letty stood tensely, watching his every move. "Going
to be a little embarrassing leaving my house bright and

early in the morning like this, isn't it, Augustine? What will the neighbors say?"

"They'll say you spent the night with your fiancé. Happens all the time these days. Even in small towns like Tipton Cove. Perfectly acceptable. Don't worry. Your reputation won't suffer." He started for the door.

"Oh, gee, thanks. Well I'll tell you something, I don't give a damn about my reputation anymore. But what about yours, Xavier?" She sprinted after him as he opened the front door and stepped out onto the porch. "What will they all say when they find out I ended my engagement after only one night with you? They're bound to think you must have been a heck of a disappointing lover if you couldn't even please a dull, boring, terribly naive little history professor."

Xavier glanced across Letty's tiny, neatly groomed front yard and saw her neighbor, the elderly Dr. Knapthorpe, Professor Emeritus of English Literature. The good professor was engaged in the process of pruning his rosebushes, which bordered Letty's drive. Knapthorpe was close to eighty but there was nothing wrong with his hearing. Xavier knew the old man was taking in every word.

"I don't know what the neighbors will think about you standing out here shrieking like a fishwife at your fiancé, Letty." Xavier strode over to the Jaguar and opened the door. "Why don't you ask them?"

He had the satisfaction of seeing her blush furiously as she realized Dr. Knapthorpe was listening.

"Beast," she hissed.

"By the way," Xavier advised as he slid into the leather-upholstered seat, "don't bother returning that wedding gown. You're going to need it when you marry me at the end of the month. Unless, of course, you find

the idea of being married in a formal gown a little too
conventional and dull for your taste. You're welcome
to show up naked at the church if you like, but one way
or another, you will be there."

"Never," she yelled after him.

But Xavier was no longer listening. He was too busy
wondering if she was really serious about taking that
suitcase full of frilly lingerie to the quarterly convention of Sheldon Peabody's Order of Medieval Revelers.

3

"HONESTLY, MOLLY, it was the most humiliating moment of my entire life." Letty shuddered.

Molly Sweet grinned cheerfully around a mouthful of anchovy and onion pizza. "From the sound of it, that isn't saying much. Apparently your life has been so blessedly bland that you haven't had any real experience with supremely humiliating moments."

"Don't remind me." Letty eyed the remains of the pizza and wondered what had happened to her normally healthy appetite.

She was usually more than capable of downing her half of the giant pizza she and Molly always ordered at this particular off-campus pub. Maybe if she sprinkled some more hot peppers on her half she could work up some interest in the dripping pizza. She reached for the bottle of crushed dried peppers.

"So he actually had you investigated? By a real detective agency? Like one of those on TV?"

"Yes. An outfit called Hawkbridge Investigations. And they didn't find one single exciting thing in my past. Twenty-nine years old, Molly, and not one event worthy of mention. You should have seen that single-page report. I could have died. Dull, dull, dull."

"I'd love to see it." Molly's eyes widened behind her glasses. "Oh, not because I'm curious about you."

"Thanks," Letty muttered sarcastically. She had to pitch her words over the sound of recorded rock music, clinking beer mugs and the noise coming from the pool table in the corner of the pub. "Apparently everyone's curiosity about me is very easily satisfied. Nothing of interest to anyone except someone looking to marry a woman without a past."

"Now, don't take offense. I just meant I'd like to see what a real background check looks like, that's all."

"Believe me, there wasn't much to it." Letty glanced up from her contemplation of the pizza and smiled reluctantly as it dawned on her that her friend was genuinely fascinated. In the subdued pub lighting she could see the intent interest in Molly's eyes.

The two young women had met shortly after Letty had arrived at Tipton College. They had discovered immediately that they had a great deal in common in terms of personal temperament, intellect and interests. They even shared a few physical similarities. Both wore glasses and both were twenty-nine years old.

Beyond those salient features, the two were quite different in appearance. Letty was a conservative dresser who favored button-down shirts with her jeans and always wore a suit and pumps to class; Molly Sweet opted for bright colors and off-the-wall styles. Tonight she had on a pair of black jeans, boots and an oversized, violently chartreuse-green knit top that glided over her slender frame all the way to her thighs. The flashy, whimsically designed earrings she wore were so long they brushed her shoulders.

Letty's dark chestnut mane was almost always anchored neatly at the nape of her neck, but Molly's golden brown hair was cut in a short sassy style that suited her vivid blue-green eyes and delicate features.

Although the two had a lot in common, their intellectual interests had taken them down different career paths. Letty's single-minded obsession with medieval studies had led her to specialize in research and teaching in the field of history. But Molly's eclectic interests together with a host of quirky enthusiasms had led her to choose a more generalized field. She was a reference librarian at Tipton College Library.

Letty picked up a slice of peppered pizza. "It gives me the creeps just thinking about it."

"What? The investigation?"

Letty nodded, wrinkling her nose as she chewed. "The thought of somebody sneaking around behind me, following me, watching my every move, making notes. It just makes my skin crawl."

"Actually," Molly said, looking thoughtful, "I would imagine there was very little, if any, of that sort of investigation. That's the way it was done years ago. Times have changed. Sometimes you spend so much of your life living in the medieval world, Letty, that I think you forget about the modern one. These days I'll bet investigations are done by computers."

"Computers?"

"Sure. The same way credit checks and reference checks are run. You can find out almost anything you want to know about someone if you know what you're doing with computers."

Letty stared at her. "You could?"

"I think so." Molly's brows rose. "Why are you looking at me like that? Is there an anchovy hanging out of my mouth?"

"No, no, I was just thinking. Molly, you know a lot about computers. You search sophisticated data bases all the time when you do research for grad students and faculty."

"Uh-huh. Academic-oriented data bases for the most part."

"But you could get into others?"

"Sure, although it's surprising what's available in the academic ones."

"Would it be illegal?"

"No. Some data bases are publicly accessible, some you pay a fee to search and, as a librarian, you'd be amazed at how many I could get into just by asking permission. What are you getting at?"

Letty put down her unfinished slice of pizza. "Could you, hypothetically speaking, run a discreet little investigation on Xavier Augustine?"

Molly's mouth fell open and she, too, put down her pizza. "Are you serious?"

"Shush. Keep your voice down." Letty leaned over the table. "Is it possible?"

Molly thought about it. "Theoretically and hypothetically speaking, yes, I imagine so. But do you think there's anything to find?"

"Probably not." Letty sat back in disgust. "The man is so noble and so terribly conscious of doing everything in the right and proper fashion that his background is probably not much juicier than my own."

Molly drummed her nails on the table. "I wouldn't be too sure of that. Xavier Augustine is a self-made man from all accounts. He didn't inherit money, he made it the hard way. Take it from me, Letty, no one gets as rich and successful as our Saint Augustine without leaving a few bodies buried somewhere along the way."

Letty turned that over in her mind. "Like some landless medieval knight who decides to make his fortune by becoming a professional mercenary."

"They did that back then?"

"Certainly. There were a lot of knights who had no fortune or land of their own. The only way up in the world was to sell their swords to some lord who needed manpower to defend his castle or raid his neighbors' property. When the mercenary had enough money and power of his own he got himself some land, selected a wife suitable to his fine new status as a respected man of property and went about siring as many sons as possible."

"A lowly, landless knight who had been able to turn himself into a powerful lord would probably have had all sorts of unpleasant little secrets in his past—" Molly observed "—human nature being what it is and all."

"You know, I'm beginning to think my knight in shining armor may be more like the original version than I initially thought. The real thing was a tough, arrogant warrior who would have done all sorts of horrid things himself, but insisted upon having a wife who had a spotless reputation."

"A little unreasonable, to put it mildly."

Letty shrugged. "Of course it was. Typically male, though, isn't it? The reasoning behind it was that a man's honor was tied up with that of his lady. If she brought dishonor on herself, he was dishonored. So he protected her honor as fiercely as if it were his own, which was very fiercely, indeed. Castration was a common punishment for a man who dared to seduce a lord's wife."

"The lord, of course, got to run around to his heart's content, though, I'll bet."

"Right. While he was watching over his wife like a hawk, he took a little time out to seduce all the pretty castle servants and the daughters of the peasants."

Molly's mouth tilted wryly. "Well, that's one thing you don't have to worry about. Xavier hasn't seduced anyone around here as far as we can tell. And in a small community like this, believe me, we'd know if it happened."

Letty groaned. "True. He hasn't even seduced me. Nevertheless, I have a hunch you're right. I doubt that Xavier Augustine is quite the saint he tries to make everyone think he is. Molly, I want you to do it. I want you to run an investigation on him."

"Why bother? You already said you were canceling the wedding."

Letty felt a wave of depression sweep over her at that thought. "I know. I guess I just want some vengeance."

"Have you considered the fact that he may be right? That you are overreacting because you feel hurt? Letty, you told me, yourself, that you loved him. Are you sure you want to give him up?"

"No," Letty admitted candidly, aware of tears welling in her eyes. She blinked them back. "But it's done. I told him this morning I was calling off the wedding. Molly, I can't marry a man who doesn't trust me. What kind of marriage would we have?"

"You might be able to teach him to trust you."

"I will not prove myself to any man, damn it. I fell in love with him and trusted him completely. I deserved the same degree of love and trust in return."

"True. But men can be a bit weird, Letty. Let's face it. They don't always think the way we do. They get all muddled up when it comes to dealing with emotions."

"I realize that, but it's just not fair. Molly, I feel so terrible. I really thought Xavier was the right man for me. I was so sure of him."

"I know," Molly said gently. "Have some more wine and pizza. You'll feel better. Are you really going to go off to one of those meetings of that society Sheldon Peabody joined last year?"

"Yes, I am."

"I'm not so sure it's a good idea." Molly looked seriously doubtful. "From what little I've heard about the Order of the Medieval Revelers, it doesn't really sound like your kind of thing."

"You're talking about the old, dull Dr. Letitia Conroy. The new fast-forward Letty is going for wider and wilder experience."

"All the same, I'm not sure how Dr. Stirling would feel if he found out his precious little golden girl, whom everyone knows he is grooming for promotion and tenure, was out carousing with a group like the Revelers. You know Stirling thinks the world of you."

Dr. Elliott Stirling, patrician-featured, silver-haired and much respected in academic circles, was chairman of the history department. He had been extremely pleased when the new assistant professor of medieval studies had begun writing papers that had gotten Tipton College's department of history mentioned in several prestigious journals.

"Stirling may have taken some notice only because I've gotten a few things published in some of his favorite journals," Letty muttered. "You know the old saying, Molly. In the academic world, it's still publish or perish. Stirling would lose interest in promoting me tomorrow if he thought I was never going to get another paper in print."

Stirling had made no secret of his satisfaction with Letty and she would have been naive, indeed, not to realize she was slated for rapid advancement at Tipton

College. Unless, of course, she blotted her copybook so badly that Stirling became annoyed.

Letty cringed inwardly at that thought. After all, until she had made the mistake of getting engaged to Xavier Augustine, her academic career had been the most important thing in her life. And there was no denying that in a small, inbred academic community such as Tipton College, the double standard in behavior still applied to a certain extent, just as it did in the modern corporate world.

The flat truth, although everyone denied it, of course, was that the social rules for men were still different than those for women, just as they had been during the Middle Ages. People might turn a blind eye to the peccadilloes of a male member of the faculty but they would frown severely on similar behavior on the part of a female faculty member.

Not that some progress had not been made in the past eight hundred years, Letty reminded herself wryly. Back in the Middle Ages women had not even been allowed to join an academic faculty, let alone given an opportunity to struggle for tenure.

"I realize Stirling is delighted with you because you've brought some prestige to the department," Molly said patiently. "You can't hold that against him. In a lot of ways he's no different than a manager in a large corporation who promotes the people under him because they made his department look good. That's the way the real world works and you know it. You can't do anything to jeopardize your career."

"I'll be discreet," Letty vowed.

"Even Sheldon has the sense to keep fairly quiet about his activities with the Revelers. No one around here really knows what goes on at those meetings he attends. All we've heard are a few rumors and I, for one, don't like the sound of them. From all accounts there's a lot of partying and general carousing."

"What's wrong with that?" Letty asked defiantly.

"It's not you, Letty."

"It is now."

Molly sighed. "I think you should reconsider the idea of rushing off to join this crowd. Find some other way to show Augustine you aren't suitable wife material."

Letty scowled. "I'm not doing this to prove anything to Xavier. I'm doing it for myself."

Molly grinned. "Don't give me that. You were perfectly content with your life until this morning. If you'd felt the need to experiment with walking on the wild side, you'd have tried it years ago. Even you must have had a few opportunities along the way. You weren't that sheltered."

Letty slapped the table with her palm, thoroughly outraged now because Molly was too close to the truth. She had been very content with her life until this morning. "It's the principle of the thing, damn it."

"Hey, hey, hey," said a jovial new voice. "Did I hear the word principle? Sounds like an academic sort of argument going on here. Nothing I like better. Mind if I join you, ladies? I need a beer, a lively discussion and some female companionship to bring me back to life. I think that last batch of exam papers I just finished grading had petrified my brain."

Letty and Molly looked up at Sheldon Peabody who was looming over the table with a hopeful, appealing expression on his handsome face.

Dr. Sheldon Peabody was thirty-six years old and rather good-looking in a soft, dissipated sort of way. His sandy hair, blue eyes and regular features gave him a boyish charm that he had used to advantage all his life.

Peabody had started to put on a little weight in recent years and had lost some of the athletic look that had been part of his attractiveness. But the slight paunch around his middle was well concealed tonight by a black pullover that he wore with his jeans.

Peabody had risen to the rank of associate professor in Tipton's history department. He had not yet gained tenure or a full professorship, however, and people were starting to notice that fact.

Gossip had started to the effect that Peabody's career advancement was stalled until he got something important into print. He had apparently fallen behind in his research and writing during the past couple of years and had not had any papers published for some time.

"You can sit down, Sheldon," Molly said politely but without much enthusiasm, "if you promise not to stick us for your beer tab the way you did last time."

"Thanks." Sheldon dropped carelessly into an empty chair and signaled the waitress for a mug of beer. "What have you got on that pizza?"

"Anchovies, onions and peppers on what's left of it," Molly told him. "I already ate my half. Help yourself. Letty doesn't seem very hungry tonight."

Sheldon eyed the remains of the pizza and grimaced. "No thanks. Even if I liked anchovies and onions, which I don't, it looks like there are enough hot peppers on it to set fire to the thing." He turned his winning smile on Letty. "Got your note in my box this afternoon. So you finally changed your mind about attending one of our little conventions at Greenslade Inn, hmm? That's great."

Letty was not sure she liked the intense satisfaction she saw in Sheldon's eyes. It made her uneasy. But she was committed now. The new Letty was trapped inside, waiting to spring free. "You've been telling me how much fun it is so I've decided to give it a try. If the invitation is still open, that is."

"Oh, it's definitely still open, my dear. I'll be glad to get you a guest membership for this quarter's convention. I'll even put your name in for full membership in the Order, if you like. About time you let your hair down a little and did some fast living. You'll have a great time. Trust me. I'll see to it personally."

"Uh, thanks." Letty hid a small shiver of apprehension. It occurred to her that this notion of attending a meeting of the Revelers might not be one of her better ideas after all. Then she thought of that single-page report that had summed up her whole life and she hardened her resolve.

"Where is this Greenslade Inn?" Molly asked coolly.

"Down the coast toward the California border." Sheldon smiled genially as his beer was set in front of him. "Great old place. It's all by itself, a couple of miles from the nearest town and it sits right on a cliff overlooking the sea. Lots of atmosphere, you know? Built by some rich timber baron back in the eighteen-hundreds. Even looks something like a castle, which makes it perfect for the Revelers. The management books the entire inn for our use while we're meeting there."

"It sounds interesting," Letty allowed.

"You'll love it," Sheldon assured her. "Say, why don't you and I drive down together tomorrow? No sense taking two cars."

Letty gnawed briefly on her lower lip as she caught Molly's narrowed glance. "I think I'd rather have my own transportation available, Sheldon. Thank you, anyway."

"Suit yourself." He shrugged dismissively and took a swallow of beer. "I'm glad you're coming but I'll admit I was a little surprised to get your note. Didn't think that new fiancé of yours would let you off the leash for something like this."

"It's none of Xavier's business," Letty said in a tight voice.

Sheldon chuckled and gave her a conspiratorial glance. "So Augustine doesn't know, huh? What is this, Letty? Eat, drink and be merry because at the end of the month you're going to be shackled to a tyrant?"

Letty swallowed. She had not yet told anyone except Molly that the engagement to Xavier was off. She drew a deep breath. "Well, Sheldon, to be perfectly blunt, there isn't going to be a marriage."

His eyes narrowed in obvious speculation. "Oh-oh," he said softly. "So that's how it is, is it? Sorry to hear that." He did not sound sorry at all. He sounded pleased.

"Pretend you didn't hear it," Xavier Augustine advised in a cold voice from directly behind him. "Because the wedding is definitely going to take place on schedule."

Letty, Molly and Sheldon swung around in surprise. Letty flinched and felt her pulse rate quicken as she saw the implacable expression in Xavier's green eyes. She told herself that anger was the emotion she was feeling, not trepidation. The man was truly overbearing. He radiated all the innate arrogance and authority of a genuine medieval knight.

"What are you doing here, Xavier?" Letty asked, sounding peevish, even to herself.

"That should be obvious. I dropped in for a pizza. Hi, Molly."

"Hi, Xavier. Have a bite. Letty obviously isn't going to finish hers."

Xavier sat down next to Letty and reached for a slice. "What the hell have you got on this thing, anyway? It looks like it's covered with hot peppers."

"It is. Also anchovies and onions. I like my pizza, as well as a few other things I could mention, very, very hot." Letty smiled with taunting innocence.

Xavier's eyebrow climbed as he nonchalantly took a large bite of the over-peppered pizza. "I'll keep that in mind." His gaze did not so much as flicker as he calmly chewed and swallowed the spicy pizza.

Sheldon scowled at Letty. "What's going on here? You two getting married, or what?"

"Yes," Xavier said around a mouthful of pizza.

"No," Letty said simultaneously. She rounded on Xavier. "Stop contradicting me."

"You're still wearing my ring," he pointed out, taking another bite of peppered pizza.

She looked down in horror and instantly yanked the emerald off her finger. How on earth could she have forgotten to remove his ring? "Here, take it. You should be able to get your money back. I'm sure a really *first-class* jeweler will be happy to refund your money."

Xavier pocketed the ring and continued eating pizza. "I'll hold onto it until you've gotten over your little problem."

"What little problem has she got?" Molly demanded, clearly intrigued.

"Bridal jitters," Xavier diagnosed authoritatively. He signaled for a beer. "Letty's suffering from a bad case of cold feet. But she'll recover."

"Maybe my feet will get warmed up this weekend," Letty threatened furiously.

"Yeah," Sheldon murmured as he took a sip of beer. "Maybe."

Xavier finished the pizza and leaned back in his chair to contemplate Letty with a detached expression. "So you're still planning on going to that convention of Revelers you told me about?"

Letty, who had been suffering serious doubts on that subject, reminded herself once more she had to stand firm. Only a very boring person would lose heart now. "Yes, I am. And that's final, Xavier. There's no point trying to talk me out of it."

"Good for you," Sheldon said, hoisting his beer mug in a mocking salute to her courage.

"I'm not going to try to talk you out of it," Xavier said mildly. "I'm planning on attending, myself."

Sheldon choked on his beer. "You can't," he sputtered indignantly. "Attendance at a meeting of the Order is by invitation only."

"So you're going to invite me, aren't you, Peabody?" Xavier smiled a dangerous smile. His eyes were green glaciers.

"The hell I am. Why should I do that?"

"Because if you don't, I will seriously consider withdrawing my commitment to endow the new chair in business administration and I will see to it that the trustees of the college know that you were the reason I changed my mind."

Sheldon's handsome face paled and then tightened with fury. He knew as well as everyone else at the table what that threat would mean. Quite literally it spelled the end of his career at Tipton College. The trustees would never forgive him for depriving the school of a major endowment. They would see to it he was fired.

"You're a real bastard, aren't you, Augustine?" Sheldon's voice was hoarse with fury.

"I can be when I'm crossed. Otherwise, I'm really very easy to get along with. Just ask anyone."

Sheldon got to his feet with a jerky movement and regarded Xavier with a frustrated hostility that was obviously just barely under control. "You think you're so damned smart, don't you? Go ahead and show up at Greenslade. I'll tell the people in charge that you've got a personal invitation from me. We'll see how much you enjoy the quarterly meeting. You don't know what you're getting into, Augustine."

"I think I can handle anything you can come up with, Peabody."

"Don't bet on it." Sheldon turned away from the table and strode through the crowd to the door.

Letty sat frozen in shock. A glance at Molly revealed that her friend was just as stunned by the outrageous threat Xavier had so casually issued as she was. Xavier himself appeared oblivious of the scene he had just caused. He was reaching for another slice of Letty's pizza.

"How dare you?" Letty squeaked as she finally found her voice.

"It's not that bad," Xavier said, regarding the peppered pizza with a considering eye. "A bit heavy on the anchovies, but otherwise pretty tasty."

"I'm not talking about the pizza. I'm talking about what you just said to Sheldon. That was absolutely appalling, Xavier. How could you threaten him like that?"

Xavier gazed at her as he munched pizza. "I hate to tell you this, but it was amazingly easy."

"My God, you're impossible." Letty shot to her feet and tossed down her napkin as if it were a gauntlet. "I have never been so embarrassed."

"You're in for a lot more embarrassment if you continue to throw Peabody and me into a ring together," Xavier warned.

"I am not doing any such thing," Letty stormed. "Furthermore, I want to make it quite clear that I don't want you at Greenslade. Do you hear me?"

"Everyone in the place can hear you," Xavier said.

Letty gave up. She glanced desperately at Molly, who got to her feet like the good friend she was and prepared to follow her out of the pub. The two women turned their backs on Xavier and stalked out of the restaurant.

"Whew," said Molly as they stepped outside into the cool night air. "I think you're right. Whatever else he is, your Mr. Augustine is no saint."

"I want you to dig up anything you can on him, Molly."

"I'll get started on it right away," Molly promised. "Should prove interesting. A man like that is bound to have lots of skeletons in his closet. But even if I find them that still leaves you with the problem of what to do with them."

"I'll think of something. I'm going to teach Xavier Augustine that he can't treat me as if he were some lord from the Middle Ages."

"Uh-huh." Molly sounded doubtful.

"I will," Letty assured her fiercely.

"Just leave me a number where you can be reached."

"I will."

Molly nodded. "I don't know if it's any consolation, but you can take comfort in knowing that we all just stuck Xavier with the bill for the pizza and drinks."

"So we did," Letty said. The thought cheered her somewhat. "I guess there is some justice in the world, after all."

THE RED MESSAGE LIGHT on the telephone was flashing when Letty was shown to her room at the Greenslade Inn the following afternoon.

"Just pick up the phone and ask the front desk for the message," the bellman said as he dropped her suitcase and took the dollar she was holding out to him. "The costumes are in the closet over there." He nodded to a wardrobe across the room. "They're provided by the Order for all new guests. Regulars bring their own and some are pretty spiffy. Cocktail party starts at six. Banquet at seven-thirty and then we batten down the hatches."

Letty blinked. "I beg your pardon?"

The bellman grinned. "This your first Revelers' meeting?"

"Yes, it is."

"Well, have fun. That's the main goal, as far as I can tell. I've worked half a dozen of these conventions and they're wild. I'll be running up and down these halls all night. You'd never think a bunch of folks who claim to be interested in ancient history would get so crazy. Some of them can be a real pain. But the tips are great. Enjoy yourself, Miss Conroy. And thanks." He closed the door behind himself.

Letty gazed around at the room with a sense of surprise and relief. She had not known quite what to expect but she was delighted with the old-fashioned canopied bed, the huge, carved wooden wardrobe and the lovely view of the windswept sea. When she walked to the window and looked down she could see the breakers crashing on the rocks of the cove below. Very picturesque. The perfect honeymoon spot, in fact. That thought made her sigh. She would not be going on any honeymoons now.

The inn was just as Sheldon had described it—a majestic old mansion built of stone and stout timber. It occupied a high bluff situated on a particularly isolated section of the coast. Two newer wings of rooms had been added on to the old section to provide additional space, but Letty was glad to discover she had been put into the original portion of the structure. Her room was on the third floor above the large rustic lobby.

Letty noticed there was a door in one wall, which meant there was a room adjoining hers. She made a note to be certain the door was locked from her side before she went to sleep later. Then she picked up the phone.

"You have a message from a Miss Molly Sweet," the desk clerk said cheerfully. "She wants you to call at once."

Frowning over the apparent urgency of the message, Letty hung up and dialed Molly's home number in Tipton Cove.

"Molly? It's Letty. Is everything okay?"

"Boy, am I glad you called." Molly's voice was laced with excitement. "Are you alone?"

"Of course."

"I mean, Augustine isn't there with you?"

"I told him he wasn't welcome, remember?" Letty said, irritated by Molly's assumption that Xavier could simply show up when and where he wished. She had seen no sign of him thus far and she was praying his statement that he would be attending the Revelers' meeting was an empty threat. "What's going on, Molly?"

"I started the search," Molly said quickly. "Just as we agreed. I've got to tell you, Letty, this is fun. I could really get into this investigation business."

"Molly, will you please just tell me what you found out?"

"Okay, okay. I plugged Augustine's social security number into every data base I could find. The first thing I can tell you is that he's healthy. Donates blood regularly."

"For heaven's sake, Molly, I already knew that." Letty was disgusted. "He was behind me in line at the last Tipton Cove Community Blood Drive, remember?"

"He's got a great credit rating," Molly offered helpfully.

"That's not exactly news. I didn't figure him to be on welfare."

"Well, if that doesn't impress you," Molly said with slow relish, "try this on for size. There is no record of Xavier Augustine existing until ten years ago."

"*What?*"

"You heard me. It looks like he invented the name and a whole new identity for himself thirteen years ago."

Letty felt as if she'd been pole-axed. "But people don't do things like that."

"They do if they've got a good reason for burying their old identity."

"Oh, my God."

At that moment, the door that connected Letty's room to the adjoining one opened and the man who called himself Xavier Augustine walked in.

4

PANIC SEIZED LETTY. For one long, stricken moment she could only stare wide-eyed at the stranger lounging in the doorway. Xavier Augustine, the stranger she had very nearly married.

"Letty?" Molly's voice sounded very far away. "Is something wrong? Are you all right? I know this is something of a shock. But it's actually kind of exciting when you think about it. I mean, there's a real mystery here. Just think, you almost married the man and you don't even know who he really is. Letty?"

"Hello, Xavier," Letty said weakly. "What are you doing here?"

"I accepted Peabody's invitation, remember?" Xavier said with patient calm. He folded his arms across his chest and leaned one broad shoulder against the door frame. His cool, brooding gaze never left her face.

"Xavier's there?" Molly yelped in Letty's ear. "Right there in your room?"

"Yes. Yes, he is, as a matter of fact." Letty's fingers clutched the receiver. "He just walked in."

"Good grief. I'd better get off the phone. Listen, Letty, be careful, do you hear me?"

"I hear you."

"Don't confront him until we know more," Molly advised quickly. "We don't know what we're dealing with yet. He could be anything, anything at all."

Letty frowned, her gaze still on Xavier. "Like what, for heaven's sake?"

"Oh, I don't know. Maybe a gangster or a jewel thief or an undercover agent of some kind. Listen, if he's a criminal he might turn violent if he knows you're on to him."

"I'll keep that in mind," Letty snapped as irritation overcame her initial panic. Molly's thinking always had an imaginative bent.

"Goodbye, Molly," she said very clearly. "Thanks for checking up on me. As you can see, I arrived safe and sound and I'm looking forward to the next few days. Don't worry, I'll give you a full report when I get back."

"Right," Molly said conspiratorially. "That's the spirit. Play innocent. Don't let Augustine know we're checking up on him. I'll get back to you when I've got more info. 'Bye."

Letty gently put down the phone and glowered at Xavier.

"That was Molly, I take it? Checking up on you?" Xavier asked.

Letty cleared her throat with a small cough. "Checking up on . . . me. Yes. Right. Me. She was checking up on me. She just wanted to make certain I'd arrived safely."

"A good friend."

"She certainly is."

Xavier smiled grimly. "So naturally she's on your side in this little war we find ourselves waging."

"Well, of course she's on my side. What other side is there?" Letty retorted.

"Mine?"

Her scowl deepened. "Don't be ridiculous." She pushed her glasses up a bit higher on her nose. "What war?"

"Haven't you noticed? You've retreated inside your castle walls and locked and barred the gate. I'm left with no option but to lay siege."

Letty blinked. "What a ridiculous analogy."

He appeared thoughtful. "Do you think so? I was rather proud of it. It seemed sort of appropriate under the circumstances."

"How would you know?" she demanded.

"Letty, my sweet, I don't claim to be an expert, but neither am I a total write-off when it comes to medieval studies."

"What?"

"I've read almost everything you've ever written and published on the subject and I'm told it's some of the best stuff being done in the field today."

That stunned her. She stared at Xavier, aware of an immediate sense of warmth at the realization that he had gone to all that bother. "You have? Everything?"

"Everything I could find."

"I hadn't realized you'd looked up all those papers." She blushed with embarrassed pleasure. "You never mentioned them. Some of them were awfully dull."

"I read every word," he assured her gently. "And I didn't find a single one of them boring."

"Oh." Then it struck her that it was undoubtedly his private investigation firm that had dug up the articles and papers she'd authored. Xavier had probably received neatly annotated summaries of each one presented to him as part of the firm's final report. Just a few more boring entries in her very boring file. The brief warmth faded. "Well, don't worry, there won't be a quiz."

"I could pass it."

"I'll just bet you could. Look, Xavier, I don't know why you felt you had to follow me here to the Revelers' convention. I assure you, it's not going to be your sort of thing at all and it's bound to be awkward for both of us."

"Not for me," he said.

"Don't be so sure," she retorted. "I understand things get a little wild around here. This is a real rowdy crowd. Party animals. Even the bellman said so."

"I think I can handle a little partying."

She eyed his unconcerned expression with a deep sense of wariness. "I hope you're not going to try to get in my way, Xavier, because I won't tolerate any interference from you. Our engagement is over and I consider myself free."

"You're not free." Xavier's voice was surprisingly gentle.

"Oh, yes I am."

He unfolded his arms and crossed the room in three long, stalking strides. He came to a halt in front of Letty and tipped up her defiant chin with one long finger. Then he looked down at her with a disturbing awareness.

"You're locked away inside your castle for the moment," he said, "but when you finally surrender and decide to open the gate and lower the drawbridge I'll be waiting to enter."

Letty went very still. She licked her suddenly dry lips. "Don't be so sure you'll want to carry out the siege. When you get to know the new me, you'll undoubtedly decide I'm not the sort of wife you want after all."

Xavier's smile was curiously enigmatic, as if he knew something she did not. "And maybe when you get to know me a little better you'll realize I'm not the sort of man who gives up something that belongs to him."

"But I don't belong to you," Letty sputtered.

"Yes, you do, Letty. You just haven't realized it yet. But you will." He brushed his lips lightly, possessively, over hers. "You will. If it's any consolation, I blame myself for the situation we're in now."

"You should blame yourself. It's definitely all your fault."

"I know. If I'd taken you to bed a month ago or two months ago instead of trying to play the gentleman, you wouldn't be so skittish now."

"Don't be too sure of that. I'd have turned very skittish the minute I saw that horrid report from the private investigators. Having me checked out as if you were thinking of employing me in a top security job was just too much, Xavier."

He nodded soberly. "My second mistake was not destroying that report after I'd read it. As I said, the present situation is all my fault. I take full responsibility."

"Stop saying that. I'm not asking you to take responsibility, I'm telling you that you should be ashamed of yourself for showing so little trust in the woman you claim you want to marry. Admit it, Xavier. What you were planning was nothing more than an old-fashioned arranged marriage to a suitable woman you had carefully chosen to meet your specifications. The way you went about the whole thing was positively medieval."

"I'd think you, of all people, would have appreciated that." There was a distinctly whimsical glint in his emerald eyes. "Given your intellectual interests, you ought to have found it romantic."

"Well, I didn't. Not in the least."

"I'll have to see what I can do to correct all the mistakes I've made lately."

Before Letty could find an appropriate response to that outrageous remark, Xavier walked back toward the connecting door. He stepped through it and closed it softly behind him.

Letty stared blankly after him for a stunned moment. Then she leapt to her feet and darted over to the door, intent on locking it securely. There was no bolt, just a simple old-fashioned doorknob lock. She pushed it firmly and heard the reassuring click.

Then she slumped in relief against the door and tried to take stock of the situation.

The thing she could not figure out was why Xavier Augustine, man of mystery, had followed her here to the Revelers' convention. Apparently he did not yet understand that she was very serious about her decision to turn around her dull, boring life. He needed to be convinced that she was soon going to be a totally unsuitable candidate for the position of wife to Saint Augustine.

Out in the hall a horn sounded and a loud voice called out, "Hear ye, hear ye. The festivities are about to begin. Sir Richard, Grand Master of the Order and Lord of Revelry for this convention, commands all guests to appear in the main hall in half an hour. Those summoned shall obey Sir Richard's command to eat, drink, be merry." Another blast on the horn followed the announcement.

Letty straightened away from the door and went purposefully toward the wardrobe to see what costumes had been provided. She was going to have fun, she vowed silently. She was going to kick up her heels and *live*. And Xavier Augustine, whoever he was, could have his fancy private investigators go find him another suitable wife.

Letty flung open the wardrobe doors and gazed at the apparel hanging inside. A small thrill of delight went through her as she reached out to touch the brilliant orange and red and blue garments. She took one gown off the hangers and examined it with a sense of wonder. Everything looked beautifully authentic, just like clothing out of a textbook on medieval costume design.

Letty made her choice for the evening and placed the garments on the bed while she took her shower. A few minutes later she stood in front of the mirror and carefully arranged her attire.

First came a *cotehardie*, a long gown with long tight sleeves and a flared skirt that moved delightfully around her ankles. It was a wonderful shade of sapphire blue and it neatly skimmed her figure, drawing attention to her slenderness. The neckline was wide and rather low. There was also a leather belt studded with bright glass jewels that rode low around her hips.

Over the long gown went a sideless jumper called a *cyclas* that was open from shoulder to hip to display the sapphire dress and the belt. The cyclas, done in panels of red and orange, had a deep neckline to show the low-cut neckline of the cotehardie.

When she had finished adjusting the gown Letty studied herself for a long moment and then decided to go for the whole effect. She brushed out her dark chestnut hair, parted it in the middle and arranged it into a heavy coil over each ear. Then she picked up a *crespinette*, an elaborate gold hair net, and put in on over the coils. She anchored the hairpiece with a gold fillet studded with blue glass gems. The fillet circled her forehead, fitting like a small crown.

Letty grinned as she surveyed herself in the mirror. She felt wonderfully medieval and altogether daring. She loved the long, graceful lines of the gown and the subtle sensuality of the cutaway cyclas. Through the opening at the sides of the garment one caught glimpses of the low, jeweled belt. It glittered and sparkled with each step she took.

The only anachronism was her glasses. Spectacles were not unknown in the Middle Ages, Letty knew, but they had been quite rare and had certainly not been worn by women of fashion. But Letty was not about to spend the evening wandering around in a fuzzy haze. She left the glasses on her nose.

Then she slipped her feet into the soft, absurdly pointed shoes that had been provided and decided she was ready for the world to meet the new Letty Conroy. Dropping her room key into a small, hidden pocket in her gown, she went out the door to try a taste of the exciting life.

LETTY STEPPED OUT of an elevator on the balcony overlooking the main lobby of the old Greenslade mansion and studied the remarkable scene below. She was instantly enchanted by the colorful medieval spectacle that awaited her.

The rustic hall was filled with laughing, chatting people in full period costume. The women were dressed in outfits similar to the one Letty wore. Some had elaborate wimples and veils held in place by small hats and fillets. The men were attired in tunics and surcoats anchored with low-slung belts. The main difference between their costumes and those of the women were that the tunics were cut much shorter, often just to the knee. Under them they wore brightly colored hose and soft pointed shoes.

Everywhere there was brilliant, gemlike color. The people of the medieval period had loved rich hues. Letty caught glimpses of fanciful heraldic devices picked out on several of the costumes and wondered if it signified some status within the Order of Medieval Revelers.

A fire blazed on the massive stone hearth that occupied one entire wall at the far end of the room. Everyone appeared to be drinking from metal or earthenware goblets. Letty decided that most of the members probably brought their own. She hoped someone had stocked a few plastic glasses for newcomers.

There was a minstrels' gallery at the far end of the balcony where she stood and several musicians in period costume were warming up the lutes, harps, flutes and drums.

The laughter from the main hall drew Letty down the grand staircase. She moved slowly, wary of the unfamiliar feel of the pointed slippers and long skirts of her costume.

Sheldon Peabody hailed her as she reached the bottom step. He elbowed his way through the throng, his goblet raised high in greeting.

"Ah, the fair Lady Letitia. Welcome, my dear, welcome to your first meeting of the Order of Medieval Revelers. May I say that the style of the times becomes you. You are truly a vision, my dear. Allow me to fetch you some wine."

"Thanks." Letty smiled in relief at a familiar face. "That sounds wonderful."

"This way, my lady." Sheldon took her arm and steered her toward a bar that had been set up against the far wall.

Letty examined Sheldon surreptitiously, noting that the green tunic he wore over yellow leggings were emblazoned with an heraldic device that appeared to be a griffin swigging a cup of ale.

"The ancient and honored coat of arms of the Sheldon family?" she asked with a grin as a costumed bartender took her order for red wine.

Sheldon chuckled. "Are you kidding? My family is from Kansas. Their symbol would probably be an ear of corn. No, my lady, this device I so proudly wear is one I designed myself. I felt it suited my particular skills."

"I should have guessed."

"To tell you the truth," Sheldon continued, "I'm hoping to replace it soon with the heraldic device of the Inner Circle of the Order of Medieval Revelers."

"What's the Inner Circle?"

Sheldon shrugged. "Basically it's the board of directors of the Order. The Grand Master this year is Richard Hodson. He's also serving as Lord of Revelry at this convention. The guy's an author. You may have heard of him."

Letty's brows rose behind the frames of her glasses. "The Richard Hodson who writes those clever mysteries set in medieval England?"

"The same." Sheldon grimaced. "The man doesn't even have a degree in history, but the editors and the public love those medieval settings he uses. Can you believe it? Makes you wonder if we're wasting our time trying to teach the real stuff to thick-headed undergraduates, doesn't it?"

"Well, I have to admit I enjoy teaching," Letty said cautiously. She had caught the underlying note of bitterness in Sheldon's voice and suspected it was directly related to his own inability to get published recently.

"You wouldn't if you'd been at it as long as I have and discovered that no one in our business appreciates good teaching. All the powers-that-be demand is a good track record in getting your papers into the right journals. It's all politics. Publish or perish, Letty."

"I understand."

"I doubt it." Sheldon's angry scowl cleared as if by magic and he gave Letty his genial, boyish grin. "But that's because you're still fresh in the game. You haven't come up against the publish or perish problem yet, have you? You're still the department's rising star."

"I don't know about that." Letty felt suddenly awkward. In an effort to change the subject, she glanced around, hoping against hope to see a familiar face in the crowd. But it was useless. She was in a room full of exotic strangers.

One of the them—a young, pretty woman with a mass of burnished gold hair flowing out from under a fillet—spotted Sheldon and started toward him. The woman's gown was cut considerably lower than Letty's and revealed a great deal of healthy cleavage. She looked to be about college age. She was fit and tan and extremely energetic. There was something in the sway of her walk and in her open, fresh good looks that spoke loudly of Southern California beaches.

"Hey, Shelly babe," the young woman exclaimed in the bright breezy accents one associates with cheerleaders, "gee, I'm glad you made it. I've been looking forward to seeing you again." She gave him a quick, proprietorial kiss on the cheek and then turned speculative eyes toward Letty. "Oh, hi there. Who's your little friend, Shelly?"

An oddly flustered expression appeared in Sheldon's eyes for a few seconds. He got control of himself quickly. "Dr. Letty Conroy, meet Jennifer Thorne." Sheldon smiled warmly at the blonde. "Jennifer's father is one of the trustees of Rothwell College. You've heard of Rothwell, haven't you, Letty?"

"Rothwell," Letty repeated thoughtfully. "Isn't that the college down in Southern California that features pictures of students playing beach volleyball on the cover of its brochures?"

"Rothwell is what is familiarly known in the trade as a party school," Sheldon said. "Isn't that right, Jennifer?"

"Like absolutely for sure, Shelly. At Rothwell we believe in having fun while you get an education," Jennifer said. She giggled and her cleavage bounced exuberantly in response.

"You're attending Rothwell?" Letty asked politely.

"For sure. I'm a senior this year."

"Majoring in history?"

"Oh, no. I'm a drama major. What on earth would I do with a degree in history? I'm going to be an actress. But I just love fooling around with medieval history, don't I, Shelly babe?"

"Er, yes. Yes, you certainly do, Jennifer." Sheldon cleared his throat and gave her a serious, confidential look. "Would you mind if we got together a little later, babe? I have a few things to discuss with Dr. Conroy."

"For sure, Shelly babe. See you later." Jennifer smiled her blinding smile and waggled her long-nailed fingers. It was apparent she did not consider Letty much of a threat. "'Bye, Doc." She swayed off into the crowd.

Letty wrinkled her nose. "Doc?"

"Hey, babe, you've got a Ph.D.," Sheldon said, clapping her jovially on the back. "Might as well flaunt it. Most of the other folks here tonight are real amateurs—dentists, stockbrokers, secretaries, all kinds of people who just happen to get a charge out of the medieval thing, you know?"

"I think that's nice. It's good to see non-academic people taking an active interest in history."

"I'll let you in on a little secret. The Inner Circle would like to attract a few more members with some legitimate academic credits. They see it as a way of raising the academic credibility of the Order. Get my drift?"

"I didn't realize the Revelers were interested in raising their academic credibility."

"Well, it's true, they're all amateurs and hobbyists, but a lot of 'em think they should get more respect from mainstream historians." He winked broadly. "Play your cards right with Sir Richard and I have a hunch you're a shoo-in for membership."

"Sir Richard? That would be Richard Hodson? The Grand Master of the Order?"

"You got it. He'd love to get a few more genuine historians on board. It would make him look good. By the way, Letty," Sheldon continued amiably, "speaking of academic credits, I read your last paper. The one on medieval marriage contracts of the early thirteenth century. Very interesting." He nodded with a wise air. "Not a bad job, my girl."

"Thank you."

"I've been wanting to discuss it with you. I detected one or two weak points, but on the whole, I believe you're on the right track. Recently I've been doing some new research in the same period and it occurs to me we ought to consider doing a joint paper on the subject of the property rights of medieval widows."

Letty sipped uneasily at her wine. The last thing she wanted to do was get involved in a joint project with Sheldon Peabody. Xavier was right. Sheldon Peabody was something of a pompous ass. She felt a bit sorry for him, but she had no intention of writing a paper with him.

"Well, medieval widowhood is a fascinating subject, of course," Letty admitted carefully. "After all, the only time a woman had any real freedom or rights to speak of during the era was after she became a widow. Until then she was under the control of either her father or her husband. But I don't think our work is focused in the same direction, Sheldon. You've always emphasized the study of medieval patterns of warfare."

"Warfare is out of fashion. Social history is the in thing these days. Family life, the role of women, that kind of thing. I've decided to explore new directions. Just think about it, Letty," Sheldon urged, his smile more charming than ever. He draped a familiar arm around her shoulders and pulled her against his side, blithely ignoring her effort to resist.

"Sheldon, I don't know. I really do think . . ."

"My lady, I have a feeling the two of us could turn out something pretty spectacular together. And I'm not talking about just a single paper, either. Hell, we might even get a whole book out of it. Yeah, pretty spectacular."

"If you don't take your arm off my fiancée," Xavier said in a deceptively casual tone from directly behind Sheldon, "something spectacular is going to happen right here in front of the entire assembled multitude of the Medieval Revelers. And it won't be pretty."

"*Xavier.*" Letty jumped at the sound of that all too familiar voice. She whirled around, recognizing the steel in it, even if Sheldon did not.

"Oh, it's you, Augustine." Sheldon's arm fell away from Letty's shoulders. "I was wondering when you'd show up. It was too much to hope you'd get lost en route, I suppose." With a bored air, he held his goblet out to the nearest bartender for a refill.

Letty fixed Xavier with a repressive frown. "Xavier, if you don't stop going around implying we're still engaged, I'm going to have to take serious measures. I really won't tolerate—oh, my goodness." She broke off in amazed wonder at the sight of Xavier Augustine in medieval garb.

He looked devastating. There was no other word for it, Letty decided. Xavier wore a stark black tunic emblazoned with a gold leopard. His leggings, boots and the shirt, which he wore under the tunic, were all black. An ornate belt rode low around his lean hips. The total effect, taken together with his riveting green eyes and midnight dark hair, was extremely unsettling.

Letty's nerve endings felt as if they'd had a close brush with electricity. She had no problem at all imagining Xavier donning a suit of armor, mounting a big destrier and riding off to do battle. She reminded herself firmly that history scholars were frequently accused of being overimaginative.

"Yes, Letty? What serious measures are you going to take?" Xavier accepted a glass of wine from one of the bartenders.

"Never mind," she muttered. "This isn't the time or place for this sort of discussion."

Xavier shrugged. "There's nothing to discuss as far as I'm concerned."

"An interesting perspective on the problem," Sheldon drawled.

"It's the only perspective. The trouble with you academic types is that you're inclined to view things from strange angles."

"So now you're an authority on the academic approach?" Sheldon's mouth tilted sarcastically and he slanted an amused glance at Letty. "No wonder you called off the wedding, my dear. Our Saint Augustine seems to think his business success is more impressive than your academic accomplishments."

"Letty knows I have nothing but respect for her academic accomplishments, don't you, Letty?" Xavier smiled at her.

Letty stared at him, horrified by the suddenly charged atmosphere between the two men. "Well, I thought you did, but I . . ."

"It's the accomplishments of one of the other members of the history faculty that leave me unimpressed," Xavier murmured.

"Why, you son of a—" Sheldon bit off the remainder of the epithet. "Damn you, Augustine, you think you can throw your weight around and get away with it, don't you? Let me tell you something. If you had the guts to fight fair instead of using your clout with the trustees to threaten me, I'd teach you a lesson you wouldn't forget."

"Hell, why not?" Xavier took a swallow of his wine. "Consider the threat lifted. I only needed it to make sure I got an invitation to this convention, anyway. I hereby swear not to use my clout to get you fired from Tipton.

If you want to teach me a lesson, Peabody, you go right ahead and try."

"Gentlemen, how dare you," Letty yelped, frantic now. "This is getting out of hand. I feel as if I'm standing between a couple of genuine thirteenth-century hotheads trying to stage a quarrel in the castle hall. Xavier, how can you act like this? It isn't like you at all."

"How would you know?" he asked softly, green eyes glinting.

That brought Letty up short for an instant. The man had a point. According to Molly, she knew nothing about him. But Letty could hardly acknowledge that at the moment. "You're a civilized, well-mannered gentleman and I expect you to behave like one."

His smile was cool and dangerous. "Is that right? I got the impression you didn't appreciate my gentlemanly behavior."

Letty felt herself turning a brilliant shade of pink as she realized he was referring to her comments on his restrained method of courtship. "For heaven's sake, Xavier."

"Besides, you wanted to spice up your life a little, remember?" he continued smoothly, paying no attention to her admonishing scowl. "Nothing like having a couple of quarreling knights stage a small duel with you as the prize to add zest to your placid existence, right?"

Letty stared at him. "Xavier, are you crazy?" she hissed. "This isn't like you. You're going to cause a scene."

"Scenes are the very stuff of the exciting life," he informed her.

Sheldon narrowed his eyes and straightened his shoulders. "Don't worry, Letty, I'll make sure Augustine here doesn't embarrass you."

Xavier turned his cold smile back on Peabody. "Now that should prove interesting."

"I'm warning you, Augustine," Peabody began, only to be interrupted by a woman's voice.

"Oh, there you are, Sheldon. I've been looking for you."

Letty and the two men turned to watch the newcomer approach. She was a plump woman with beige hair who appeared to be in her late forties. She was attractive in a hard-edged kind of way. Her gown was dark blue and fuchsia. She was wearing a transparent veil over the back of her hair that was anchored in place by a fillet. When she reached Sheldon, she slipped her arm through his and smiled at Letty and Xavier.

"Hello," she said with a bright salesperson's smile. "You must be new. I don't recognize you and I know almost everyone at these conventions. I'm Alison Crane. From Seattle. I'm in real estate. High-end condos mostly. I do a fair amount of business among the Revelers. Here, let me give you a card."

"Uh, Alison, this is Dr. Letitia Conroy from Tipton College," Sheldon said quickly as Letty automatically extended a hand to take the business card.

"I'm Xavier Augustine," Xavier said blandly when it became apparent Sheldon was not going to bother introducing him. "No, thanks. I don't need a card. I'm not planning on buying any real estate in Seattle in the near future. But I'll keep your name in mind."

"How do you do?" Letty said, grateful for the opportunity to defuse the quarrel that had been building between Xavier and Sheldon. "You've been attending these conventions for some time?"

"Ever since they started five years ago," Alison assured her. "Made some great contacts here."

Letty looked at her. "That's why you come? To make business contacts?"

"One of the reasons. But history was my major when I was in college and after I graduated I turned it into a hobby. Just like most of the other people in this room. Something fascinating about medieval history, isn't there? I subscribe to a couple of major academic journals and I believe I've read one or two of your articles on women's roles in the Middle Ages, Dr. Conroy. Fascinating stuff. Absolutely fascinating."

"Thank you," Letty said, quite flattered. "Please call me Letty."

"Certainly. You know, you really ought to consider writing a book on the subject of medieval women aimed at the non-academic market. Your writing style is extremely readable. Not in the least dry or pedantic. I should think there would be a sizable market."

Sheldon looked sage and thoughtful. "What a coincidence. Alison, I was just telling Letty that she and I should get together to collaborate on a book, wasn't I, Letty?"

"Well," said Letty, feeling pressured again and wishing she could think of a polite way out of the situation. "I don't know, Sheldon. I mean, I've never tried anything for the popular market. I'd want to do a lot of thinking before I committed myself to anything like that."

Xavier stepped closer to Letty in a move that emphasized his claim on her. "Forget it, Peabody. If Letty wants to write a book, she'll do it on her own. She doesn't need a collaborator."

"Why don't you get lost, Augustine?" Sheldon threw him a scathing glance and took another gulp of his wine.

"Don't hold your breath, Peabody. I'm not going anywhere without Letty."

Letty was mortified.

Alison's smile went up another couple of watts as she serenely ignored the byplay between the two men. "Do think about it, Letty. I'm sure you would do a wonderful job. Now, if you'll excuse me, I've got to run. I see an old client of mine over in the corner. Oh, by the way, I'm having a little after-hours get-together in my suite after the official festivities are finished tonight. Drinks are on the house. Room 209. Come on up, if you get the chance. Both of you. And you, too, Sheldon. You always do."

Alison floated away through the crowd in search of her ex-client and Letty watched her go with a pang of regret. She did not like being left alone with Xavier and Sheldon.

But before she was forced to deal with the two quarreling knights, a horn sounded from the far end of the hall. A man dressed in the costume of a page held up a large scroll and cleared his throat.

"'Hear ye, hear ye, me lords and ladies. All members of the Order of Medieval Revelers are hereby summoned to the grand banquet. Sir Richard shall lead the way.'"

"Listen, Letty," Sheldon said earnestly as the crowd surged toward the banquet hall doorway, "I'll be eating at the head table. I'd like to ask you to join me up on the dais but there wasn't time to make arrangements for tonight's meal. Your decision to come to the convention caught me by surprise."

"That's quite all right, Sheldon," Letty said quickly. "Don't worry about it, I'll be fine."

"Right," said Xavier, taking her arm. "She'll be fine. She'll sit with me."

Sheldon smiled thickly at Xavier. Then he shifted his gaze quickly back to Letty. "Enjoy yourself, Letty. I've arranged a little surprise for you toward the end of the banquet when the jongleurs show up." He turned and got swept up in the throng.

"What are jongleurs?" Xavier asked.

"Traveling minstrels. It was fashionable for the knights to write poems to their ladies. They often had the jongleurs set them to music and sing them. Haven't you ever heard of troubadour poetry?"

"I think I read about it in one of your papers. A lot of nonsense about some idiot knight pining away for a lady who won't give the guy the time of day, right?"

"In a nutshell. You're such a romantic," Letty said.

"Don't I get any bonus points for trying? Let me tell you something, Letty, I wouldn't dress up in this funny outfit for just any woman."

5

NO DOUBT ABOUT IT, Xavier thought midway through the lavish feast, he had definitely screwed up when he had inadvertently allowed that investigation report to fall into Letty's hands. He still did not completely understand why she had gotten so upset but she had. And he was paying for his carelessness now by having to sit through this crazy parody of a medieval banquet.

The scene that confronted him was downright bizarre as far as Xavier was concerned. The room had been draped in heavy tapestries depicting scenes of hunting, warfare and other events of medieval life. Everywhere there was color and outrageous pomp. Women in fancy headdresses and brilliant gowns were seated next to men dressed in tunics, tights and pointy shoes. Several of the men wore odd caps made out of felt. Gaudy jewels that anyone could see at a glance were fakes, gleamed in the belts and glittered from the head wear. The laughter and chatter was getting louder and more raucous as the wine glasses were refilled. It was a damn good thing nobody was driving home tonight, Xavier decided.

The diners were seated at two long rows of tables that extended out from the head table. Harried-looking waiters and waitresses garbed as pages and serving wenches scurried back and forth with huge platters of food.

Sheldon Peabody and several other high-ranking Revelers were all sitting under a yellow and white striped canopy on a raised platform at the far end of the room. Although he pretended to ignore them, Xavier was fully aware of the frequent glances Sheldon sent toward Letty who was clearly enjoying herself immensely.

Xavier had to admit that his lady did look lovely in her strange gown and the silly gold hair-net she was wearing. The little circlet of metal that went around her head like a delicate crown gave her a regal air. It only went to prove that true class showed regardless of what a woman wore, Xavier told himself proudly. Letty would look good in anything.

Tonight there was a captivating, otherwordly charm about her that made him want to pull her close and protect her from Peabody's lecherous gaze. Xavier sipped his wine and idly wondered how many medieval ladies went to banquets wearing glasses.

"What's wrong?" Letty demanded in a low voice. She shot him a sidelong glance as he narrowed his eyes over the wine. "You don't approve of the Burgundy, Sir Xavier?"

"It isn't a genuine Burgundy. It's a cheap California red."

"My, my, how depressing for you. But you seem to be holding up manfully under the stress of having to drink cheap wine."

"Yeah." Xavier took a closer look at her strange hair-style.

"What are you smiling at?" Letty asked irritably as she helped herself to more vegetables.

"I was wondering what you'd done to your hair. It looks like you're wearing ear muffs." Xavier continued to examine the rich, dark chestnut coils that gleamed inside the gold net.

"I'll have you know this style was the *height* of fashion in the late Middle Ages."

"Is that right? What was the *depth* of fashion?"

"The codpiece," she informed him with grim relish. "It came into vogue at the end of the medieval period and truly flowered, one might say, during the Renaissance. Be grateful your costume is from the fourteenth century. If it had been from the fifteenth you might have had to wear one and somehow I just can't see you in a codpiece."

Xavier wondered if she was actually teasing him. If so, it was a good sign. "You don't think I could have managed to fill one out properly?" he asked politely.

"Nobody actually *filled out* a codpiece," Letty said sweetly. "At least not by virtue of natural endowment. The men stuffed them with cotton wadding or something."

Xavier grinned. "Sort of like putting tissue inside your bra, I guess." He was rewarded with a hastily muffled giggle from Letty. "Would you mind passing me the peas?" he continued. "Looks like I'll have to eat them with my spoon. Have you noticed there aren't any forks on the table?"

"Forks weren't around in medieval times," Letty explained. "People used spoons and knives and fingers. At least we've got real plates. In the old days they used trenchers made of large slabs of stale bread to hold the food. And there would have been rushes down on the floor to catch the stuff that got spilled. And lots of dogs running around under the table, of course."

"The local health department probably put its foot down when the Revelers applied for a permit for rushes and dogs in a public restaurant. We should all be grateful. I assume most of this food is not particularly authentic, either."

"Well, there isn't any larded boar's head or roasted peacock, but other than that a lot of it would have looked familiar to a medieval diner. The main difference between the food we eat now and what people ate back then is in the preservation and preparation techniques."

"I suppose they were a little short on refrigerators and freezers."

"Right. But they were very good at concocting thick, rich sauces and gravies to cover up food that was past its prime. And they had all sorts of exotic spices, some from the Far East. They routinely cooked with ginger and cloves and cinnamon. Some of the recipes were incredibly complex." Letty paused and then smiled in delight. "Oh, look, here comes the entertainment."

Xavier glanced up and saw a team of jugglers dressed in green and orange costumes with whimsical pointed caps. They were taking up positions in the middle of the floor between the long tables. The crowd roared its approval as the entertainers began tossing soft colored balls into the air.

"Xavier, are you really intending to stay here the whole four days?" Letty asked bluntly, her eyes on the jugglers.

He contemplated her profile, trying to figure out what she was thinking. "If that's what it takes."

She turned her head, eyes flashing behind the lenses of her little glasses. "If that's what it takes to do what? Just what is it you expect to accomplish? I'm not going to change my mind, you know."

He sighed and leaned back in his chair, hooking his thumbs in his low-slung belt. "Letty, two days ago you were in love with me," he reminded her gently. "I don't think anything has changed. You're just feeling a bit anxious. You'll get over it."

"This is not a case of bridal jitters, Xavier Augustine. I am angry and hurt and I will not be changing my mind. Don't give yourself any false hopes."

He smiled wistfully. "All I've got left is a little hope, sweetheart. Would you take that away from me along with everything else?"

She blinked and then her brows came together in a fierce expression. "Don't you dare try to make me feel sorry for you. I don't believe for one minute that you ever really cared deeply for me. Go find another suitable wife. I'm out of the running."

"Not yet," he drawled, wanting to laugh at her determination to move into the fast lane. "You haven't done anything to disqualify yourself yet."

"I will."

"I doubt it. You're too damned smart to do anything really stupid just to spite me."

She slammed her knife down on the table. "You're insufferable."

"Just desperate. I want you very badly, Letty."

He watched the blush rise in her cheeks as she glanced around hurriedly. She was obviously afraid that someone on either side of them might be eavesdropping. Xavier could have told her not to worry. Everyone else was either laughing at the jugglers' antics or talking loudly to his or her neighbor. For all intents and purposes, Xavier and Letty might have been alone in the crowded room.

"Stop talking like that," Letty muttered as she sank her small white teeth into a chunk of dark bread.

Xavier leaned closer to murmur in her ear. "I'm sorry you were upset by that investigator's report. I never meant to hurt you."

"Then why did you pay someone to spy on me?"

He frowned. "It wasn't exactly spying."

"Yes, it was."

"All I can say is that I had my reasons."

She turned to him with glittering eyes. "What reasons?"

Xavier contemplated her for a long moment, wondering how much to tell her. Damn, what a mess. But it was clear Letty was going to demand some answers from him. "It's a long story, love. And it has nothing to do with us."

"The hell it doesn't."

Xavier started to argue that point but was interrupted by another annoying blast from a horn followed by a monotonous drumming. He looked around to see that the jugglers had retired and had been replaced by a group of musicians dressed as minstrels.

"Now what?" he growled.

"The jongleurs," Letty said, looking expectant. "This should be fun."

One of the musicians stepped forward and held up his hands to call for silence and attention. When he had it he removed his belled cap and bowed deeply to the room full of people.

"My lords and ladies, I beg you to listen to the song I am about to sing for you. Pray remember that I am but a messenger, a humble servant of the bold knight who has commissioned me to convey his deep admiration for his fair lady. His only plea is that she listen to his heartfelt words of appreciation for her beauty, grace and form."

A round of applause greeted this announcement and the jongleur stepped forward to stand directly in front of Letty. Xavier saw her eyes widen in pleased surprise. She glanced toward the dais and Sheldon Peabody inclined his head with what was probably meant to be knightly grace.

"Damn," Xavier said beneath his breath. Out of the corner of his eye, he saw Peabody preen beneath the yellow and white canopy as everyone clapped again. It did not take much guesswork to figure out which bold knight had arranged for this performance. One of these days, Xavier decided, he was going to have to do something about Dr. Peabody.

The minstrel began to strum his lute and sing in a slow, mournful style. Xavier lounged in his chair and drummed his fingers impatiently on his belt.

Oh, I would tell you of my lady fair;
She with the dark flames burning in her chesnut hair
Ye shall hear of her radiant gaze, of eyes that glow like crystal pools;
Of lips as sweet as fine spiced wine and of how she breaks this heart of mine.
Each part of her is sheer perfection; each more beauteous than the rest
Oh, how I shall languish until I am free to kiss her noble brow and caress her fair, white breast.

Rage boiled in Xavier's veins as the last lines of the song sank home. When they did, he leapt to his feet.

"*Caress her fair, white breast,*" he roared. "Who the hell do you think you are, Peabody? Nobody, and I mean *nobody*, talks about my fiancée's fair, white breast except me."

"Xavier," Letty hissed, tugging frantically on his sleeve, "Xavier, please, sit down. It's troubadour poetry. They always sing about breasts and eyes and hair. Sit down, for heaven's sake."

Xavier ignored her, his whole attention on Peabody's mocking smile. "I want an apology, Peabody. And I want it now."

"You want me to apologize?" Sheldon looked amazed. "Why on earth should I apologize to anyone? What you have heard is nothing more than a humble tribute to a beautiful, intelligent, utterly charming woman."

"It's a damned insult, that's what it is, you bastard. And you will apologize, by God." Xavier planted one hand on the white cloth and vaulted lightly over the table.

He landed easily on the floor in the middle of the room and started striding toward the platform where Peabody sat. The musicians scrambled out of the way, a couple of them tripping over their long pointed shoes. The crowd hushed.

"Xavier, what do you think you're doing?" Letty called out anxiously. "Please come back here. You're causing a scene."

"I don't give a damn about embarrassing Peabody," Xavier declared, aware that the entire assembly of Revelers was watching in stunned silence. "He deserves it for embarrassing you."

"But I wasn't that embarrassed," Letty said in a small voice. "Honest. It was just a poem, Xavier."

Xavier paid no attention to her weak protests. He'd had enough of Sheldon Peabody. He came to a halt in front of the head table and reached out to sweep aside the dishes and trays of food behind which Peabody was barricaded. Platters, goblets, knives and trays cascaded across the white tablecloth.

"What the hell?" Peabody leapt to his feet as wine trickled into his lap. "What do you think you're doing, Augustine?"

The other diners seated under the canopy quickly edged out of the way, but made no effort to halt the scene. It was apparent the crowd was beginning to enjoy this new sport.

Sir Richard, a large, florid-faced man in his late forties, picked up his knife and rapped on his goblet for attention. "I see we have a little matter of chivalry and honor to settle here. It would seem these two bold knights both seek the attention of the same fair lady. What say you, my lords and ladies? How shall we deal with this?"

"Let them both compose poems and we'll all sit in judgment tomorrow," yelled one man dressed in a red and gray tunic. "The winner gets to entertain the lady tomorrow night."

"Let the lady choose between them," a woman in a high, wide headdress and veil suggested.

"Aye, aye, let the lady choose," Alison Crane echoed. "It's her right."

"I say we let them compete for her," someone else suggested. "Let them engage in an archery contest or a chess match."

"No, a quest. Make it a quest."

"Yes, a quest. Let's stage a quest." The cry was echoed around the room and accompanied by loud applause.

Sir Richard rapped his goblet once more. "As Lord of Revelry, I must make the choice and I shall have to think on the matter." He turned toward Xavier and Sheldon. "Do you prefer archery, chess or a quest, sir knights?"

Xavier looked at Peabody. "What I prefer to do is wring Dr. Peabody's neck until he apologizes for insulting my future wife."

Peabody turned a dull red. "You think you can do it, Augustine? Go ahead and try." He leaned over the table, his expression viciously taunting. "Just go ahead and try. But be warned, I've studied with a master in the martial arts."

"I'll keep that in mind." Xavier put his hands on Peabody's shoulders and hauled him bodily across the table. Then he released him.

Peabody squawked loudly as he fell in a heap at Xavier's feet. "How dare you treat me like that? I'm going to wipe the floor with your face, Augustine. You'll pay for this."

Xavier stepped back out of reach as Peabody jumped up and lashed out with his foot. Xavier caught hold of the other man's ankle and yanked. Peabody went back down on the floor, rolled to one side and climbed back up to his feet. He looked murderous.

Xavier risked a quick glance at Letty and saw the horrified expression on her face just as Peabody lunged forward.

"You think you're so smart, Augustine? Try this on for size," Peabody bellowed. He swung wildly, a huge, roundhouse punch that was obviously a mile off.

Xavier considered Letty's expression and abruptly changed his mind about his tactics. He had been intending to pound Peabody into the floor but another strategy now beckoned. He gritted his teeth and waited for Peabody's fist to connect.

When it finally did with a dull, smacking sound, Xavier rolled with it so that the impact was not nearly as bad as it looked. But he made the most of it.

Amid startled shrieks from the audience, he crumpled magnificently to the floor and sprawled full-length at Peabody's feet.

For a moment no one in the room moved. Xavier looked up at Peabody through slitted lashes and realized the man was uncertain what to do next.

Peabody stood over his fallen victim, looking as surprised and confused as everyone else in the room at first. But that expression was soon replaced by a look of pompous satisfaction as it dawned on the professor that he had just vanquished the challenger in a single blow.

"I warned you, Augustine. Don't say I didn't warn you," Peabody crowed.

It was Letty who broke the stunned tableau. "*Xavier.* Oh, my God, Xavier, what has he done to you?"

Xavier lay still and listened contentedly to the sound of crashing dishes and silverware as Letty leapt out of her seat and scrambled over the table to get to him. He sighed in satisfaction as he heard her softly slippered little feet pattering madly across the floor and then she was crouching at his side, touching him with anxious, gentle hands.

"You've hurt him, Sheldon. How could you? Look at him, he's unconscious. You might have broken some bones or given him a concussion. Someone call a doctor. Hurry." She touched Xavier's bruised lip and cheek. "Speak to me, Xavier. Wake up, darling, and speak to me."

"Don't call a doctor," Xavier mumbled. "I'll be okay."

Relief flared in Letty's worried eyes. "Thank heavens, you're not unconscious. I was so frightened. Does it hurt very much?"

"A little," he admitted, opting for the stoic touch. "But I'll probably feel a lot better once I start the lawsuit proceedings."

"*Lawsuit.*" Peabody's voice was suddenly several notches higher. "Now see here, Augustine, you've got no right to sue me. You started this."

"Did I? My memory is a little foggy at the moment." Xavier rubbed his jaw. "Probably a result of the blow."

"I've got a hundred witnesses, damn it," Peabody retorted. "Tell him he hasn't got grounds for a suit, Letty."

"No one's going to sue anyone," Letty said soothingly as she put an arm under Xavier's shoulders and helped him sit up. "You were both at fault. But you shouldn't have hurt him like that, Sheldon. That sort of violence was uncalled for."

"He started it, damn it," Sheldon yelped.

"Well, I know, but all the same, physical violence is never the answer," Letty reminded him primly. "Are you sure you don't need a doctor, Xavier?" she added in concern. "You look a little odd."

"I'll be fine," he said bravely as he stifled a laugh. "But I'd like to go upstairs and get a cold compress on my jaw, if you don't mind. I've heard it's good for keeping the swelling down."

"Swelling. Good heavens, yes. You need to get a compress on that jaw immediately. I'll help you. Lean on me, Xavier." She staggered under his weight as she assisted him to his feet. When he swayed, she gripped his waist and tugged his arm around her shoulders. "Be careful, darling."

"Thanks, honey," he said weakly. "Sorry to disrupt the festivities. I'm sure no one will mind if we leave now." Over the top of Letty's head he smiled a victor's smile at Peabody whose eyes narrowed in sudden suspicion.

"He doesn't need any help, Letty," Peabody said.

"I'll be the judge of that," Letty informed him with fine hauteur. "You should be ashamed of yourself, Sheldon."

"But, Letty..."

"So long, Peabody," Xavier said. "See you around. Hey, no hard feelings, big guy. I had it coming." He raised the hand that was resting on Letty's shoulder and waved good-naturedly. "Win some, lose some."

Sheldon's face turned purple. "Letty, don't get suckered in by this jerk. He's not badly hurt."

She glared at him as she eased Xavier toward the door. "Don't try to tell me he's not hurt, Sheldon. I saw you hit him. You knocked him down. It was dreadful."

"He walked straight into it—deliberately, I'm beginning to think," Sheldon muttered as he hurried along beside her.

Xavier groaned in pain and leaned more heavily on Letty's shoulders. She responded by pulling him closer and giving Peabody another furious glance.

"I saw it all," Letty announced. "You knocked him down, Sheldon. Now please get out of my way. I have to get him upstairs so we can apply cold compresses."

"Damn it, Letty, I'm telling you..."

"Telling me what?"

Peabody groaned and gave up. "Never mind." He gave Xavier another narrowed glance. "You think you're so damn smart, don't you, Augustine?"

"Who, me? I don't have a Ph.D. like you, Peabody. How could I possibly be smarter than you?"

Peabody started to reply to the taunt but at that moment a well-endowed young woman with acres of blond hair bounded forward out of the crowd.

"Hey, Shelly babe, are you all right?" The young woman grasped Peabody's arm. "That was just super, the way you decked him. Like absolutely awesome. I've never seen anything like it. Wow. You really flattened him. Totally. Are you sure you're all right?"

"I'm fine, Jennifer."

"That was a really super song you wrote. Some people just don't appreciate real talent." Jennifer shot a cool glance at Letty.

"Not now, Jennifer," Peabody muttered, his frustrated gaze still on Xavier.

The banquet hall door closed on Sheldon Peabody's twisted grimace of frustrated fury. Letty did not appear to notice. She was too busy guiding Xavier across the lobby.

"I can't believe what happened in there," she said as she steered her charge into the elevator and punched the button. "Two grown men brawling over the banquet table."

"Welcome to the exciting life."

She glowered. "Xavier, this is not a joke. You could have been seriously injured."

He hung his head and tried to look chastened. "I know. I was a fool. I just couldn't handle it when I heard that verse about caressing your fair, white breast. I went a little crazy. Hell, Letty, even I haven't caressed your fair, white breast."

"Neither has Sheldon Peabody, so don't get upset," she retorted. "Honestly, Xavier, I told you it was just a song in the tradition of the medieval style of chivalric love. The knights who wrote the poems sang a lot about longing to caress their ladies, but the fundamental principle of chivalric love was that it was platonic and unrequited. The ladies weren't supposed to actually respond."

"Don't try to tell me Peabody was only thinking of worshipping you from afar when he wrote that damned song for you. And don't tell me you weren't responding. You were enjoying that stupid poem."

She had the grace to blush. "Well, it is the first time anyone ever wrote a poem to me, I must admit."

"It was an insult, by God."

"Listen, Xavier. You want to talk about insults? I'll tell you right off that I was a lot more insulted when I found out you'd had me investigated than I was hearing I had fire in my hair and fair, white breasts."

Xavier recognized a bad strategy when he saw one. He retreated quickly, groaning loudly and rubbing his jaw. "Ow. Sure hope Peabody didn't loosen any of my teeth."

Letty immediately stopped berating him and started fussing nicely. "I can't believe Sheldon hit you. How dare he? He always seemed like such a nice, civilized sort of person. This is so unlike him."

"Uh-huh."

Xavier considered going back down to the banquet hall and shoving Peabody's teeth down his throat. Common sense overrode male hormones, however. After all, Xavier told himself, he was the one alone up here with Letty. Peabody was downstairs, no doubt stuffing himself at the head table and wondering why the fair lady had left with the loser.

Xavier grinned faintly at that thought. Obviously Peabody was better at writing stupid love songs than he was at understanding how women like Letty thought.

"What's so funny?" Letty eased Xavier off the elevator at the third floor and started down the hallway.

"Nothing. Just a grimace of pain."

"Oh, dear." She looked up anxiously. "Is the pain getting worse?"

"I'll survive. I think." He searched for the pocket in the strange clothes he was wearing. "Here's my room key."

She took it from him and opened his door. "I have never been so shocked in my whole life as when you leapt over the table and went to confront Sheldon." She switched on the light and helped him sit down on the edge of the bed. "I've never seen two men fight before. It was sickening."

"It's even more sickening to lose."

"Who could have guessed Sheldon would have turned so violent? Just be grateful you weren't hurt any worse than you are." She went into the bathroom. "Stay where you are. I'll fix up a compress."

"Thanks." Xavier listened as she ran water into the sink. He caught sight of himself in the mirror and winced at his grim image. Dressed entirely in black with his dark hair rumpled and nursing a split lip he was probably not a maiden's delight.

"Here we go." Letty came out of the bathroom with a damp washcloth neatly folded into a compress. "Lie down and I'll adjust it."

Xavier did as she directed and leaned back against the pillows. The folds of her brightly colored gown wafted around him as she bent to apply the compress to his bruised jaw. Surreptitiously he inhaled the delightful scent of her as he gazed at the expanse of skin exposed by the low neckline of her costume. Her hands were wonderfully gentle as she dealt with his wounds.

"Thank you, Letty," he murmured. "That feels much better."

She frowned. "You're sure a cold compress is enough? You don't want me to drive you into town to the emergency room?"

He shook his head and smiled faintly. "No. I'll be fine. I'm sorry I embarrassed you."

"I suppose it's not your fault that you aren't very familiar with the traditions of medieval poetry and songs."

"I overreacted."

"Yes, you did, but it's understandable." She smiled suddenly as she adjusted the compress. "Actually, now that I think about it, your reaction could be seen in a somewhat noble light. I mean, you did think you were defending my honor in a way, didn't you?"

He watched her from beneath half-lowered lids. "I'm glad you understand."

Her smile widened and her eyes warmed. "I'll let you in on a little secret, Xavier. It could have been worse. A lot of medieval verse is a great deal bawdier than what you heard tonight. Lots of sexual allusions to battering down castle gates and plucking roses from well-guarded towers. The poems were full of tales of knights inventing ways to sneak into ladies' bedchambers. They were an earthy bunch back in those days."

Xavier scowled. "I don't think I want to hear about it. If Peabody tries to sneak into your bedchamber, I really will throttle him. *Ouch.*" He touched his sore lip.

"Sorry. Did I hurt you?"

He gave her a sharp glance and saw only innocence radiating from her concerned gaze. "No. It's my fault. I should have moved a little quicker when Peabody threw that punch."

Letty started to say something but broke off at the sound of high-spirited shouts out in the hall. They were followed by laughter, footsteps and a couple of distinctly feminine squeals. "Sounds like things are getting into high gear out there, doesn't it? Sheldon said this was a real party crowd."

Xavier experienced a moment of panic wondering if Letty was planning to join the others as soon as she had finished tending to his wounds. "I don't think I'll be up to any more fun and games this evening. I'd better keep the cold compress on this face of mine."

"Yes, I suppose so." She sounded uncertain. "Do you think you'll be all right up here by yourself?"

Xavier shook his head doubtfully and groaned. "You never know about the after-affects of a punch like the one Peabody landed. Takes a couple of hours to see if there's going to be any real problem."

"It does?"

He nodded. "Right. I'll just sit up here and watch TV by myself. You go off and have fun. That's what you came for, isn't it?"

"Well, yes, but I feel bad about leaving you up here alone watching television while everyone else is having a great time."

"I've spent worse evenings, believe me. Run along and enjoy yourself, Letty. Don't worry about me. It wasn't your fault I got beaten up."

She stood up abruptly. "I will worry about you and that's all there is to it. And it is my fault you're hurt. At least, in a way it is. Sort of. Tell you what. I've got a deck of cards in my room. Why don't we play some gin or something?"

Xavier smiled slowly. "That's very kind of you, Letty."

"I'll get the cards."

Xavier waited until she had gone through the connecting door before he picked up the telephone and called room service.

"I want a bottle of your best champagne, no, not the California sparkling wine, the real thing. From France. What have you got?" He listened to the limited selection available in the inn's cellars as it was reeled off. Then he chose the best label on the list. "And two glasses. Oh, yeah, send up a tray of snacks. Something classy. Got any good pâté or caviar?"

"Yes, sir, we do," the room-service waiter responded. "Which would you prefer?"

"Send up both."

"Right. We're getting real busy down here, sir, but we'll take care of your order as soon as possible."

"Do that." Xavier put down the phone with a sense of satisfaction. He ignored the shrieks and shouts of laughter that were getting louder out in the hall. He was going to see to it that Letty enjoyed a very private party right here in this room tonight.

He intended to show her she did not need Sheldon Peabody and his Order of Medieval Revelers in order to spice up her life. And while he was at it, he also intended to show her in no uncertain terms that all his male equipment worked just fine.

6

A LONG TIME LATER Letty put down yet another winning hand of cards and smiled triumphantly at Xavier who was stretched out on the bed, shoulders braced against the pillows.

"Gin," she announced with glee. "Again."

"I'm obviously out of my league here." Xavier folded his cards. "My only excuse is that it's getting hard to concentrate with all that racket going on out in the corridor."

The din from the corridor had increased during the past two hours. There were parties going on in nearby rooms and people were bellowing down the hall at friends or laughing uproariously. The sound of footsteps and loud music filtered through the walls.

"The bellman who showed me to my room said they battened down the hatches around here after the official festivities were over for the evening. I think I'm beginning to see why." Letty shuddered and picked up her glass of champagne. "It sounds wild out there, doesn't it?"

Xavier, apparently unfazed by his sixth losing hand in a row, put down his own cards and picked up the bottle of champagne to refill his glass. "It sure does. Sorry you're missing out on it?"

She sighed. "To be perfectly honest, no. I'm beginning to wonder if I really fit in with this crowd, Xavier. It was fun dressing up in these costumes and I did enjoy the banquet, at least I did until you and Sheldon started brawling."

"Sorry about that."

"But," she continued, "I'm not sure I would enjoy those after-hours parties going on out there. I'm not certain I would know what to do at one, if you know what I mean."

"Maybe you tried to move into the fast lane a little too quickly," Xavier said with a slow, sensual smile. "You're not used to this kind of life-style."

That observation annoyed her. "What do you suggest I do? Go back to my humdrum, boring existence in Tipton Cove? No thanks."

"I wasn't going to suggest anything so dull." Xavier covered her hand with his own, his fingers strong and warm.

When she raised her eyes to meet his, Letty drew a sharp breath at the glittering sexuality in his hooded gaze. She had seen hints of that very masculine, very exciting expression before in his eyes when he had taken her into his arms. But Xavier had never followed through on the subtle promise that had always sent shock waves through her. In the past he had always carefully disengaged himself, said good-night and left her to her lonely bed.

"No," Letty said quite firmly as she snatched her hand out from under his. "No, absolutely not."

"No, what?" His gleaming gaze narrowed briefly as he dropped his hand to rest possessively on her thigh.

"No, you are not going to do it to me again, Xavier Augustine. I've had it with your passionate good-night kisses that never go anywhere. You're not going to get me all hot and bothered again tonight and then send me off to my own room. So don't even bother to try." She stood up quickly and stepped back from the bed.

Xavier did not move. "Who said I was going to send you off alone to your own room this time?"

"It's what you did all those other times you kissed me good-night. I'm not taking any chances. You've set me up once too often. I'm calling it quits before you even begin this time."

He got to his feet with lazy grace and caught her gently around the waist. "Tonight will be different, Letty."

"I doubt it. Let go of me." She batted ineffectually at his hands as he pulled her close against his hard, lean length.

"Letty, you still love me, don't you?" He brushed his mouth lightly over hers. "You can't possibly have fallen out of love with me in the space of only two days."

"Want to bet?"

"I want you, sweetheart. I've wanted you all along." He wrapped his arms tightly around her and simply held her close, making no effort to kiss her again. He tenderly pushed her head down onto his shoulder. "And I'm through trying to play the gentleman."

"I told you, it's too late to try to seduce me." Her voice was muffled against the fabric of the tunic. "The engagement is off, Xavier. Over. Finished. Terminated."

"All right," he said thoughtfully.

Letty went very still. She hadn't expected him to agree quite so easily. A niggling disappointment shot through her. "All right?" she repeated blankly. "You mean, you're going to stop running around telling everyone I'm just suffering a bad case of bridal jitters?"

"I'll run around telling everyone we're having an affair, instead. How does that sound?"

"An *affair?*" Letty planted her palms against his chest and shoved herself back a few inches to look up into his face. "What on earth are you talking about? We're not having an affair."

"Why not?" He smiled slightly as he cupped the twin coils of hair over her ears. He held her that way as he kissed her brow. "You want to do something exciting, don't you? Why not have an affair?"

"With you?" She felt dazed. Her mind whirled as she tried to take in what he was saying.

"Naturally. Who better to have an affair with than the man you once loved enough to marry? So much safer than picking up a stranger these days. After all, you already know a lot about me. And you like me. We're compatible in lots of ways. What better basis for an affair? Hell, it was good enough to get us engaged, wasn't it?"

Letty stared up at him, belatedly remembering the phone call from Molly Sweet. "But I don't know all that much about you."

"Sure you do. You knew enough to agree to marry me." Xavier's eyes glittered with sexy humor. "If you have any questions, you can always check my references."

"References?"

"Certainly. Starting with the trustees of Tipton College. If that's not enough for you, I'll be happy to provide you with a list of my business associates. Will that do?"

Molly's words came back. *There is no record of Xavier Augustine existing until ten years ago.* Letty wondered what Xavier would say if she asked for a list of people who had known him for longer than ten years. But she did not dare to bring up the subject or demand explanations until Molly had done more re-search.

Letty did not want to look like a fool if it should turn out that Molly had simply not done a proper search on her computers. Perhaps further inquiries would reveal that Xavier Augustine could easily be traced right back to his date of birth. No, better to keep quiet for now.

Besides, she had other problems at the moment.

"Well, Letty?" Xavier eased the gild fillet off her head and removed the crespinette. He dropped the golden hair-net on the bed. Then his fingers moved in the coils of hair over her ears, loosening them.

"Please, wait, Xavier. I have to think. I don't under-stand what you're doing." Letty tried to catch his hands and failed. Her hair tumbled free around her shoulders as she looked up at him with a disconcerting mixture of apprehension and desire. She felt the fierce, wild rush of longing she always experienced when Xavier took her in his arms but she told herself she had to stay clear-headed.

"I'm starting an affair with you." His hands moved beneath her hair and his fingers caressed the nape of her neck. "Doesn't that sound exciting?" He slanted his mouth across hers in a slow, erotic kiss. "Doesn't that sound like a real change of pace?" His tongue teased her lower lip. "Doesn't that sound like a way to completely alter your life? Turn it around? Add some spice?"

"I'm not sure," she said slowly.

"Please, darling. No more insults aimed at my viril-ity. I don't think my ego can take it."

Letty was swamped with guilt. She hugged Xavier urgently. "I didn't mean to insult you. Really, I didn't. It's just that I'm trying to think my way through this whole thing."

"That's the old Letty talking. The new Letty doesn't think her way through to a decision. She surrenders to the moment."

"But I hadn't planned on having an affair. At least not with you," Letty explained baldly.

He winced. "I thought you promised there would be no more insults."

"I just meant I never expected you to be interested in having an affair with me," she amended hastily. "You certainly never showed much interest in having one in the past."

"I was a fool. Since you're bent on calling off the marriage, I no longer have much choice, do I? I've decided that an affair is exactly what I want. Can't you see that it's the perfect solution for you, too?"

"I don't know." She was still doubtful although her pulse was beating strongly now and her stomach was doing tiny flip-flops.

"Let me convince you." Xavier eased the jumperlike cyclas off over her head and dropped it down onto the bed. Then he searched out the fastenings of the sapphire-blue gown.

Letty stirred uneasily. She circled his strong wrists with her fingers and looked up at him anxiously. "Xavier, are you sure you want to do this?"

His mouth curved in an unreadable smile as he framed her face with his hands. "Trust me. I know what I'm doing."

"Oh, Xavier. I'm going to do it. I'm going to surrender to the moment." Letty flung her arms around his neck as the last of her qualms fell away. She did love Xavier. "I can see your point perfectly. Who better to have an affair with than the man I once loved enough to marry?" She lifted her face eagerly for his kiss.

"You're right. I can see that now. An affair is the perfect answer."

"I thought you'd see the light. I think we'll use your bed. It's larger. And I like the canopy, don't you? Very romantic."

"Oh, yes. Very."

He laughed, a low, husky sound that sent ripples of excitement down her spine. Then the room spun around Letty as Xavier picked her up in his arms and carried her through the open connecting door into her room.

He stood her on her feet beside the canopied bed and removed her glasses. He set them down on a bedside stand and slowly eased her out of the blue gown. Letty held herself very still, mesmerized by the compelling eroticism of his touch. His hands were strong and sure and gentle. When the archaic dress pooled at her feet, she stepped out of it, suddenly aware of the scraps of lace covering her breasts and the bit of silk that shielded her secrets.

"The trousseau lingerie?" Xavier smiled as he unclipped the bra.

"Yes. I bought it for our honeymoon," she admitted, wondering why her eyes were suddenly filled with tears.

"Don't cry, darling." He kissed away the drop of moisture that squeezed out of her closed eyes. "Think of this as our wedding night."

She sniffed back the tears as raucous laughter echoed out in the hall. "No, I'll think of it as the first night of our affair. Which is exactly what it is."

"Whatever you want, sweetheart. We'll talk it out in the morning."

"There's nothing more to discuss, is there?" Letty looked up at him, feeling an odd sense of regret.

"Yes, there is. But now isn't the time. Hush, love."

"But, Xavier..."

Xavier was no longer paying any attention to her words, however. His mouth was moving over her cheek, seeking out the tender skin behind one ear. His teeth closed briefly around her earlobe and Letty gasped.

"You're trembling," he whispered.

"I can't seem to stop."

"I'm a little shaky, myself," he admitted with a small smile as he freed her breasts. "I've waited a long time for this night, Letty."

"No one said you had to wait," she reminded him a bit irritably, even as her nipples tautened beneath his thumbs.

"I know, I know. It's my own damn fault. I make mistakes once in a while, but I always take care of them."

There was an unexpectedly hard edge in that statement. Letty raised her head to search his face but all she could see in the shadows were his gemstone eyes. They glittered with a powerful desire that took away her breath.

"Fair, white breasts," Xavier murmured wonderingly. "You are very lovely, sweetheart. You set my blood on fire. Do you know that? I was afraid to touch you like this before because I knew you'd have this effect on me. I knew that once I'd started making love to you, I wouldn't be able to stop."

"Oh, Xavier, I wanted you so." She swayed against him, clinging to his waist and resting her head on his broad shoulder.

"I'm glad. I'm very, very glad you wanted me like this." Xavier's hands slid down her bare back to the base of her spine and then closed around her rounded buttocks. He squeezed gently and groaned deep in his chest when Letty shivered. "I'm burning up, love. I'm going to bury myself in you until you put out the fire. There is no other way this time. No cold shower in the world would work tonight."

"Good." She kissed his throat. "I'm glad."

Xavier released her. He leaned down to pull back the covers on the canopied bed and then he swept Letty back up into his arms. When he deposited her in the center of the bed she instinctively reached for the sheet and pulled it up to cover her breasts.

Xavier watched the movement with hungry eyes as he undressed beside the bed. "Shy?" he whispered.

"A little."

"You'll get over it. I'm going to touch every inch of you and then I'm going to kiss every place I've touched. By morning you won't know the meaning of the word shy."

She watched him toss aside the black tunic and shirt. The sight of his smoothly muscled chest made her ache deep inside. She held her breath as he shed boots and leggings. Then Letty's eyes widened as she caught sight of his gloriously aroused body.

Xavier chuckled softly as he came down beside her. "Why are you looking at me like that, sweetheart? Measuring me for a codpiece?"

She licked her lower lip as his heavy thigh settled over her bare legs under the sheet. "No, of course not. But I must say you, uh, certainly wouldn't need any additional padding in order to fill one out," she managed, trying for a light, sophisticated tone.

His eyes softened knowingly. "Don't worry, Letty." He bent his head to kiss her shoulder. "I'm going to fit perfectly inside you."

"I'm not so sure about that."

"I am."

Xavier tugged the sheet free of her clutching fingers and pulled it slowly down to her waist. His mouth followed the receding line of the sheet, moving with slow heat across her sensitized skin. When his teeth settled tenderly around one nipple, Letty stopped worrying about whether she and Xavier would fit together properly. She just knew he was going to be perfect for her.

She arched herself against his mouth, her fingers tightening in his night-dark hair. Hot, liquid excitement poured through her and she realized she and Xavier were made for each other. She had known that since the day she had met him.

His hands moved lower, sliding over curves and hollows; seeking out her feminine secrets. When his fingers found the inside of her thigh, she moaned and sank her teeth into the skin of his shoulder.

"I knew you were going to be a passionate lover," Xavier said with deep satisfaction. His hand closed over the damp, flowering place between her legs. "So hot and sexy and wet. Sweetheart, I want you. How I want you."

"Yes. Oh, yes, *please*."

"Touch me." Xavier's voice was thick now. He caught hold of one of her hands and dragged it down the length of his body.

She felt her fingers glide through crisp, curly hair and then she was touching his sleek, powerful shaft. It throbbed beneath her fingertips as she gently circled it.

"Ah, no. Wait, honey. Bad idea." Xavier sucked in his breath and eased her hand away from himself. "Too much, love. Another couple of seconds of that and I'll explode and I want to be inside you when I do that."

She smiled mistily up at him as it finally dawned on her that she had as much power in this encounter as he did. Her hands trailed lovingly over his hip and flattened on his back. "You're so strong and so sleek," Letty whispered in soft wonder.

"And I'm about to go out of my mind. Tell me that you want me, sweetheart." His fingers slid gently inside her and then withdrew very slowly.

Letty gasped, shivering in response. "I want you. More than anything else in this world."

"Take all you want, love."

And then he was moving, pulling her gently beneath him and settling himself between her legs. The sounds out in the hall faded into the distance. Letty was aware of nothing except the need to have Xavier inside her, to be joined with the man she loved. She clutched at his shoulders, her nails biting into his skin and her whole body started to tighten.

"Easy, honey." Xavier's fingers slid into her warmth again, testing her readiness. "You're so small. I don't want to hurt you."

"You couldn't hurt me. You'd never hurt me." Somehow she was utterly confident of that.

"No, never."

He parted her gently and fitted himself to her. His mouth closed over hers and with a slow, steady, inevitable stroke he filled her completely.

Letty moaned in reaction to the tight, full feeling. But the small sound was lost in Xavier's mouth. She held herself very still as her body adjusted to the delicious invasion and then Xavier began to move.

The rhythm of his lovemaking was slow and deep and unbelievably sensual. The reality of making love with Xavier was far more thrilling than the fantasies she had entertained during the past few months. She had not realized how exciting the sheer weight of him would be as he lay on top of her. She could not have imagined the effect his curly chest hair would have on her tight nipples. She had not understood how the sexy, masculine scent of his body would tantalize her.

But most of all she had never been able to conjure up in her dreams the blazing heat that now sent her senses soaring. She had not even guessed at the sheer intensity of the experience.

Xavier's lovemaking was just like Xavier, himself— hard, strong and fiercely tender. She felt incredibly safe and protected even as her senses were being pushed to the limit.

The passion consumed her. Something inside Letty twisted tighter and tighter with each long, filling stroke. Then Xavier was reaching down between their bodies, finding her, touching her, tormenting her until she could stand it no longer. She was lost.

"Xavier."

"Yes. *Yes.* All of it. All of it, sweetheart. Give it to me."

The tension was released all at once in a gentle explosion that sent ripples all the way down to Letty's toes. Somewhere in the middle of the haze, she heard Xavier's hoarse shout of satisfaction and he wrapped her so tightly to him she could barely breathe.

Eventually Letty was aware of Xavier collapsing heavily on top of her, his body slick with sweat. He muttered something low and deep in her ear but she could not make out the words. It was too much effort to ask him to repeat himself. Besides, she did not really want to talk right now. Her emotions were confused and disjointed. Nothing was clear. Things were not quite what they were supposed to be tonight.

This should have been our wedding night, Letty thought. Instead she was starting an affair with the man she had once planned to marry.

"Letty?" Xavier's voice was a dark, velvet whisper.

"Yes?"

"Everything's okay now, isn't it?"

She did not understand what he meant. Instead of answering, Letty put her arms around Xavier's sleek back and held him close. For a long while she lay quietly listening to the noisy revelry going on outside her room and then she fell asleep.

THE SOUND OF THE PHONE ringing beside her bed brought Letty awake the next morning. She was aware of the unfamiliar sensation of a hard, muscled, masculine leg lying alongside her thigh. Then she opened her eyes and found herself staring up at the equally unfamiliar sight of a canopy over her bed.

Memory came back in a blinding flash.

The phone rang again and the heavy leg shifted. There was a loud clatter and a muffled curse as Xavier reached out for the receiver.

"Who the hell is this?" he demanded irritably as he finally got the phone to his ear. "If it's you, Peabody, you can take a flying . . . What? Oh, hi, Molly. No, you haven't got the wrong room. What do you mean—*who is this?* It's me, Augustine. Who did you think it was?"

Letty sat up clutching the sheet to her breasts and reached for the phone. "Here, let me have that, Xavier. It's for me."

Xavier gave her a slow smile filled with lazy sensuality and smugness. "She's right here, Molly. I'll put her on." He handed the receiver to Letty who scowled briefly at him.

"Molly?"

"Letty, is that you?" Molly sounded alarmed. "What's going on there? It's seven o'clock in the morning. What's Augustine doing in your room? Did he spend the night with you?"

Letty propped up a pillow and leaned back against it, aware of Xavier idly listening to every word of her side of the conversation. "Well, yes, as a matter of fact, he did."

"Good Lord, the engagement's not back on or anything, is it?"

"No." Letty avoided Xavier's possessive gaze. It was harder to ignore the big hand stroking her thigh. "No, nothing has changed."

"But you're sleeping with him? Letty, I'm not so sure that's a good idea. Things are getting curiouser and curiouser."

Letty drew up her knees and wrapped her arms around them. She slid Xavier a speculative glance which he ignored. "What's happening, Molly?"

"Remember I told you there's no record of any Xavier Augustine matching the description or social security number of your Xavier before ten years ago?"

"I remember." A small shiver went down Letty's spine.

"Well, I assumed he changed his name legally so I went looking for some record of that and you'll never believe what I got back."

"What?"

"A query," Molly said, sounding really excited now. "Somebody wants to know why I'm asking for information on Xavier Augustine."

"I don't understand. You mean someone knows you're . . . uh . . ." Letty broke off uneasily, sliding another quick glance at Xavier who finally began to take some interest in the conversation. "Someone knows you're doing some research?"

"Right. Which means that someone set up a few traps in the system to catch anyone who might come looking. A very clever someone. Letty, this could mean anything. I don't know what to tell you to do. We could be opening up a real can of worms here. I can try ignoring the query and try coming at the problem from some other direction. But I don't know what will happen. Do you want me to continue the investigation?"

"Yes," Letty said stoutly, "go ahead."

"This could be serious stuff, Letty. We may be dealing with anything from the mob to the government."

"Oh, my God."

"I know. Very mysterious." Molly echoed Letty's grim tone but underneath it, the thrill of the hunt was clearly bubbling. Molly was enjoying herself.

"Molly, this isn't dangerous or anything is it?" Letty whispered into the phone, turning her head away from Xavier's increasingly watchful gaze.

"I don't think so. Not at this stage. I don't think anyone could figure out where the search is originating and even if someone did, he'd only know it was somewhere in Tipton College. It could be anyone who happened to sit down at one of the dozens of computers here on campus."

"Just be careful, all right?"

"Listen to who's talking. You're the one who's sleeping with the mystery man, for heaven's sake. Try following your own advice."

"Yes, I will. Goodbye, Molly." Letty handed the receiver back to Xavier who replaced it without taking his eyes off of her.

"Anything going on here I should be aware of?" Xavier folded his arms behind his head, leaned back against the pillows and studied Letty intently.

"No. No, nothing at all." Letty reached for her glasses and slid them on. She peered at Xavier, thinking that he had never looked quite so raffish and dangerous as he did this morning. "Molly was just chatting about some project she's working on. She's very excited."

Letty knew her voice was much too high and thin. To conceal her agitation, she made a production of getting out of bed, trying to take the sheet with her.

"Hold it, Letty. Come back here." Xavier halted her efforts to escape by gently taking hold of Letty's arm and pulling her back down onto the bed.

She gave up the useless struggle and tried a bright, unconcerned smile. "Something wrong, Xavier?"

He glazed thoughtfully down at her. "This is the second time Molly's called since you arrived yesterday afternoon. I know you two are close friends, but this is a little ridiculous. Is she that worried about you being here?"

Letty seized on the excuse. "Yes, I'm afraid so. She wasn't at all sure I should accept Sheldon's invitation, you see."

Xavier considered that explanation and then shook his head. "No, there's something else going on here. You sounded as concerned about Molly as she was about you. Come to think of it, you've acted strangely both times you've talked to her since we arrived. What's up, Letty?"

Letty decided hauteur was her best line of defense. She sat up again and lifted her chin. "Honestly, Xavier. I don't see that it's any of your business. Molly and I were having a private conversation. It has nothing to do with you."

"Interesting."

She narrowed her eyes. "What's interesting?"

"I've never seen you try to tell a lie before. You don't do it very well, Letty. Probably haven't had enough experience," he concluded complacently.

Letty was stung. "Is that right?" she retorted rashly. "I suppose you've had plenty, haven't you?"

Something cold entered his gaze. But his voice was dangerously soft. "I've had plenty of what? Experience telling lies? Is that what you're saying?"

Too late Letty realized she had stepped into very deep water. She made another leap for freedom, dragging the sheet with her, and finally managed to stand up beside the bed. "Forget it. I was just annoyed. I hate it when you tell me how naive and prim and proper I am. I've told you, I'm changing my image."

"Letty..."

"Now, if you'll excuse me, I'd like to take a shower and get dressed." She fumbled with the sheet, trying to wrap it around herself so that Xavier would not have an unrestricted view of her derriere as she headed for the bathroom. "There are a couple of seminars I'd like to attend this morning and I want to have breakfast first."

"Letty, you're dithering."

"I am not dithering." She was suddenly enraged at the unfair accusation.

"I'm not going anywhere and neither are you until you tell me the real reason Molly called yesterday and again this morning."

Letty stared at him, furious with his implacable attitude. "I don't owe you any explanation, Xavier Augustine."

"The hell you don't. We're engaged."

"We are not engaged," Letty howled.

His eyes grew as cold as the bottom of a green sea. "You're still saying that after what happened between us last night?"

"We started an affair last night. We did not reinstate our engagement," Letty shouted as she edged backward toward the bathroom. The sheet trailed along the floor. "I thought you understood that. It was your idea, damn it. Remember? 'Why not have an affair with the man you love, Letty?' 'What better way to move into the fast lane?' Nice and safe, you said."

"Do you?" Xavier asked softly.

"Do I what?" She was feeling totally confused and agitated now.

"Do you still love me?"

"What do you care?" She was almost at the bathroom door. Another couple of steps and she would be safe.

"I care a lot, as it happens." Xavier got up off the bed, utterly heedless of his own nudity, and started to stalk toward her. "And I want some answers, Letty. What was that phone call all about?"

"Why should I tell you?"

"Because you're not leaving this room until you do tell me," he stated calmly.

"All right," Letty snapped as she reached the safety of the bathroom doorway. She lifted her chin proudly, the sheet still clutched to her bosom. "I'll tell you what it was all about. I'm checking up on you, Xavier Augustine. I'm finding out just who you really are. After all, if I'm going to have an affair with you, I ought to know a little something about you, don't you think? A woman in my position can't be too careful."

"Checking up on me? What the hell do you mean? What's Molly got to do with this?"

"She's running an investigation on you through her library computer system," Letty informed him coldly. "The same sort of investigation you ran on me. Fair's fair, Xavier."

"An investigation? On me?" Xavier's eyes were colder than ever and there was no trace of warmth or gentleness left in the lines of his fierce face.

"That's right." Letty was genuinely scared now. She had never seen Xavier in this mood. She grabbed the trailing edge of the sheet and yanked it through the doorway. Then she slammed the bathroom door in his face and locked it. "And I'll tell you something else," she yelled through the wood. "Molly has already found out some very interesting facts about you, *Saint* Augustine."

"Like what?" Xavier roared back.

"Like the fact that you didn't even exist until ten years ago." Letty experienced a brief satisfaction at the realization that she had finally managed to gain the upper hand over Xavier Augustine.

And then Xavier's fist slammed against the door, rattling it on its hinges.

Startled, Letty leapt back and stumbled over the commode. She found her balance and stared wide-eyed at the locked door.

"Xavier?"

But there was no answer, only an ominous silence from the outer room.

7

XAVIER PACED his room, fighting to keep his emotions under control. He had closed the connecting door to Letty's room because he was very much afraid if he saw her when she at last ventured out of the bathroom, he would lose his temper completely. He had not been this angry in a long, long time.

And he had never before in his life been this scared.

Letty was having Molly Sweet run an investigation on him. He could not believe it. Of all the nerve. Of all the sheer, unadulterated female gall. Who the hell did she think she was?

She was a lady bent on vengeance, that's what she was. She was doing to him exactly what he had done to her.

Xavier came to a halt at the window and stood looking down at the sea. Letty was getting even. And in the process she might get more revenge than she even dreamed. She might destroy the new life he had built for himself.

He had obviously made a very big mistake when he'd hired Hawk to run a check on his future bride, Xavier decided grimly. Everything he had worked for, everything he had planned so carefully was coming apart before his very eyes because of that investigation.

And last night he had been so certain that he'd repaired the damage he'd done, so sure he had her back in the palm of his hand again. Letty had given herself to him completely, surrendering so sweetly, so beautifully that he had felt dazed. Making love to her had been more satisfying than he had ever imagined and he was certain he had satisfied her, too. She had burst into flames in his arms.

But now she claimed she not only had no intention of conducting anything more serious than an affair with him, she was checking out his past, just as he had hers.

Unlike hers, however, Xavier knew his past could not withstand close scrutiny.

The real question here was just how good was Molly Sweet with a computer? How clever could one little librarian be, anyway?

Taking advantage of the fact that Letty was in the shower, Xavier came to a decision. He turned away from the window, dropped into a chair and picked up the phone. When he got an outside line he dialed a number from memory.

His call was answered on the second ring.

"Yeah?" The familiar voice was dark, male and thick with sleep.

"Hawk? You awake?" Xavier's fingers tightened on the receiver.

"No. I'm sound asleep. Damn. Is that you, Augustine? I've been trying to get hold of you. Where the hell are you?"

"At a little inn on the Oregon coast," Xavier explained impatiently. "Hawk, is something going on with my old files?"

"Someone's asking questions, pal." There was no more sleep in Hawk's voice now. "Don't know how he got this far, but he did. Must have gotten lucky. I tried to call you last night and got no answer. What's going on? Anything serious? This doesn't look like a routine credit check."

Xavier sighed. "You'll never believe it. My fiancée has got a friend of hers searching a computer for information on my background. This friend has already managed to find out I didn't exist until ten years ago."

"No kidding?" Hawk was clearly impressed. "That's fast work. Who is this friend? He's good. I'll give him that much."

"Her name is Molly Sweet."

"Yeah? A woman?"

"She's a librarian at Tipton College and I don't care how good she is. I want her stopped."

"I sent back a query asking for identification but she backed off immediately. Then she apparently went offline for the night. I didn't get any more responses when I tried to coax her back."

"I don't think she's going to give up. Not as long as Letty is giving the orders. You can handle it?"

"I'll try. But it might be simpler to just tell your sweetheart the truth."

"No," said Xavier. "Not yet. I've got enough trouble at the moment as it is."

"What kind of trouble?"

Xavier rubbed the back of his neck. "She's trying to call off the wedding. Claims she just wants to have an affair."

"Our sweet, prim and proper little Dr. Conroy has called off the wedding and opted for an affair instead?" Hawk gave a crack of laughter. "I don't believe it. What brought this on?"

"She found the investigation report you worked up for me and she hit the roof," Xavier admitted, feeling like an idiot because it was all his own fault. "At first I think she was merely insulted. But then she decided she didn't like the fact that her whole life could be summed up on one page of paper so she's decided to change her image."

"Your little scholar has cut the strings and decided to run wild, is that it?"

"I'm glad you're finding this so damn funny, Hawk. I don't."

"No, I can see that." Hawk made an effort to get his laughter under control. "So where are you now? Chasing after her?"

"Yes." Xavier's voice was clipped. "We're having a wild four-day weekend at a convention of medieval history enthusiasts."

"A convention of history buffs? That's your lady's idea of running wild? In that case, I wouldn't worry too much, if I were you, Augustine. How much damage can she do fooling around with a bunch of history enthusiasts?"

"You don't know this crowd," Xavier told him with great depth of feeling. "I've already been in one fight since I got here. Some jerk from the Tipton College history department wrote Letty a love poem and had it sung in front of the whole crowd. I took exception."

Hawk chuckled. "I'd like to have seen that. So what did you do? Stomp him into the roast beef platter?"

"Hell, no. I let him take one good swing and then I went crashing to the floor like a felled ox. Letty's the kind of woman who always empathizes with the underdog."

"That figures. So you played wounded warrior and let her tend your bruises, huh? Good move."

"It's not over yet. She's still talking about having an affair instead of getting married and she's still got Molly

Sweet hunting up information on me. Listen, Hawk, I don't need any more complications right now, understand? I need time to soothe Letty's ruffled feathers. I'll tell her whatever she wants to know after I've got a ring on her finger."

"What difference would that make? She can walk out on you just as easily after she's married to you as she can now."

"Not Letty," Xavier said with great certainty. "Marriage vows still mean something to women like her. Once we're married there will be a time and place to tell her everything. But I don't want to try to explain it all now. I don't trust the mood she's in. Her father was a judge, for crying out loud."

"She knows there's a mystery now," Hawk pointed out thoughtfully. "There's no stopping a woman once she senses a mystery. She'll want answers."

"I'll figure out something."

"This," said Hawk, "should be amusing. You know something Augustine? When I ran the investigation on her, I decided your Dr. Letitia Conroy sounded like a very nice lady. Now she's beginning to sound like a very intriguing lady. I always did like a little spirit in a woman."

"You can say that because you're not the one having to deal with the problems caused by a woman with a 'little spirit'," Xavier growled. "I liked Letty just fine the way she was."

"How about the way she's turning out to be now?" Hawk asked gently. "Still like her?"

Xavier blinked as it struck him quite forcefully that the word *like* did not begin to cover the way he felt about Letty today. None of his emotions toward her now could be labeled with bland words such as *like*. She was driving him crazy this morning even as his body was still basking in the afterglow of last night. He wanted to yell at her for having the nerve to investigate him but he also wanted to take her into his arms and kiss her senseless.

"As a matter of fact, I don't like her much at all right at the moment," Xavier muttered. "I'm mad as hell at her. But the woman belongs to me now, whether she knows it or not, and I'll deal with her. I'll take care of things on this end. You just do something about Molly Sweet."

"I'll see what I can do to satisfy Ms. Sweet's curiosity without giving away your dark secrets," Hawk promised. "Good luck with your courtship. You still planning the wedding for the end of June?"

"You better believe it." Xavier hung up the phone and told himself to start thinking carefully and clearly. He had a problem on his hands.

LETTY DID HER BEST to keep her attention on the young man giving the lecture on medieval methods of training falcons for the hunt. The speaker was a young veterinarian who had made falconry a hobby and he certainly knew his material. Normally Letty would have been extremely interested in what he had to say.

But Letty's thoughts kept going back to Xavier's lovemaking during the night. When she did manage to get them momentarily off that subject they leapt instantly to the scene that had taken place in her room that morning following Molly's phone call.

"A good falconer was expected to be part veterinarian, part trainer and full-time nursemaid to his valuable birds," the lecturer informed his audience.

Everything had felt so right last night, Letty recalled sadly. She and Xavier had come together so beautifully—she just knew they had been meant for each other.

"The first stages of training were carried out in a darkened room," the speaker was saying. "Nervous birds are more easily handled in darkness. The falcons were first taught to perch on a human wrist and then gradually introduced to the hunt."

Letty gave a start as someone sat down in the empty chair beside her. She did not know whether to be relieved or alarmed when she realized it was Sheldon Peabody. Sheldon was dressed in a short, dark green surcoat over light green hose. He wore a jaunty little felt cap that matched the surcoat and a pair of shoes with points that extended a good six inches beyond his toes.

"Hi, Letty," Sheldon whispered, "I've been looking all over for you."

"Good morning, Sheldon." Letty glanced at him warily. Sheldon had a distinctly pained expression on his handsome face. She frowned. "Are you all right?"

"Yeah, sure. A little too much partying last night. But I'll live. Things got a little crazy there toward the end. Jennifer Thorne insisted on demonstrating her idea of what a medieval cheerleader's routine would have been like."

"I can just imagine Jennifer leading the cheering squad at a fourteenth-century tournament."

"It does boggle the mind, doesn't it?" Sheldon agreed thoughtfully.

Up on the stage the lecturer continued his talk. "The falcons were highly valued and their training carefully supervised. A lord's favorite bird often slept on a perch in the same chamber as its master. Hunting was more than just a sport for the medieval lord, it was a way of life that perfectly complimented his half civilized, half warrior lifestyle. Society saw itself mirrored in the hunt."

Sheldon leaned closer. "Come on, Letty, let's get out of here. This is basic stuff. You're not going to learn anything new about falcon training from this guy. Let me buy you a cup of coffee. Lord knows I need one."

"I don't know, Sheldon. I really did want to hear some of the lectures."

"Forget the lectures. They're just an excuse for the partying that comes later. Everyone knows that. Besides, I want to talk to you." He took her arm and urged her to her feet.

Letty reluctantly allowed herself to be led out of the room. She and Sheldon slipped through the doors at the back and started toward the downstairs café. Letty kept an eye out for Xavier but there was no sign of him.

A few minutes later she found herself sitting opposite Sheldon near a huge window that overlooked the sea. The morning fog was just beginning to lift, revealing craggy cliffs and the vast expanse of the Pacific.

"Better," Sheldon breathed in relief as he took a long swallow of coffee. "Much better. What a night. One down and three more to go. How's the wounded victim?"

Letty studied her coffee. "Xavier's all right."

"Glad to hear it," Sheldon said dryly. "Quite a performance he put on last night."

"He really was hurt, Sheldon. You cut his lip and there was a bruise on his jaw," Letty flared, feeling obliged to defend Xavier for some obscure reason.

"He set me up, knowing that you'd fly to his side the minute he took the fall." Sheldon shook his head. "The guy's a lot sharper than I gave him credit for in the beginning, I'll admit that. I guess it's the business shark in him. But I'm still surprised at you, Letty. I thought you were smart enough to see through him."

"I'd rather not discuss this, if you don't mind." Letty made a move to get to her feet.

"Hey, sit down. Take it easy. I'm sorry." Sheldon reached out and caught her arm, urging her back down into the chair. "I apologize. For everything." He gave her a crooked, endearing little smile. "You can't blame me for feeling a trifle annoyed with the whole situation. After all, I've been doing my best to get your attention for the past year and I've hardly made any headway. Augustine walks into Tipton Cove and you fall at his feet without a murmur."

"It wasn't like that," Letty insisted, knowing perfectly well that it had been exactly like that.

"Maybe not, but it sure seemed that way. I thought maybe you'd come to your senses when you told me that the engagement was over. But after the way you left with him last night, I guess nothing's changed."

"The engagement *is* over," Letty declared, feeling pressured.

Sheldon gave her a skeptical look. "Really?"

"Really."

He nodded thoughtfully. "Well, then, there's hope for me, hmm?"

"Sheldon, please, I'm not ready to discuss another relationship," Letty said in a choked voice. She turned to gaze out to sea, wondering frantically how to put a halt to Sheldon's overtures.

"I understand. Ending the engagement must have been traumatic."

"It was."

"He didn't understand you, Letty. How could he? His background is very different from yours. You two had nothing in common."

Letty's head snapped around. "What do you know about Xavier's background?"

Sheldon's shoulders rose and fell in a negligent shrug. "Just what everyone else knows. He comes out of the business world. I know he drives an expensive car and wears smart clothes but you're not the type to be impressed by that kind of superficial glitter. You need someone from the academic world. Someone who's intellectually oriented the way you are."

She sighed and turned her attention back to the sea. "I don't know what I need at the moment."

Sheldon smiled his charming smile and touched her hand as it lay on the table. "You need someone like me, Letty. And I need someone like you. I've been increasingly aware of that for the past few months. The feeling has been growing slowly but surely. We could be a great team, honey. We have so much in common."

"Sheldon, I said I don't want to talk about another relationship right now." Letty grabbed the most convenient excuse at hand. "It's too soon. I hope you understand."

"Of course." His expression was one of sincere concern and deep understanding. "You're a very sensitive creature. You need time to recover. But you're going to have to watch out for Augustine. He's as crafty as the devil, Letty. Don't let him manipulate you the way he did last night."

"I can handle Xavier," Letty declared stoutly.

"Okay, okay. I get the point. You're a big girl." Sheldon smiled again. "I know you can take care of yourself. I admire your independence, really I do. But you can't blame me for feeling protective."

Letty groped for a way out of the uncomfortable conversation. "Thank you, Sheldon, but I'm quite capable of managing my own life. Now, I'd better be on my way or I'll miss the lecture on the construction of medieval kitchens."

"It's all elementary stuff, Letty, just like the lecture on falconry," Sheldon said impatiently. "I told you, strictly amateurs giving the talks to show off their hobbies. You won't learn anything you don't already know. Why don't you and I start talking seriously about doing a book together? Alison Crane was right when she said we could turn out something interesting. What do you say we have lunch later and discuss the idea?"

"I'll have to check my schedule." Letty rose quickly and flashed Sheldon a bright smile as she fled the café.

It occurred to her that for a woman who had until recently enjoyed an extremely dull love life, she was certainly picking up steam in that department. Last night she'd begun—and possibly concluded—an affair with one man and this morning she had another male breathing down her neck telling her he thought he was falling for her.

All things considered, Letty decided, she was definitely living a more exciting existence these days. She had actually begun to accomplish her goal of leaving her boring life behind.

She wondered why the whole thing was making her so uneasy. Apparently this sort of life-style took some getting used to.

XAVIER HAD STILL NOT sought her out by the time Letty
joined the rest of the Revelers and a small crowd from
the nearby town on the inn's front lawn. A medieval fair
had been set up on the grass. Dressed in another of the
costumes she had discovered in her room, a yellow
gown and a crimson surcoat with a white hart embroidered on it, Letty strolled leisurely around the stalls.

Now that the fog had vanished, the day had turned
out warm and summery. Brightly hued pennants and
banners snapped in the light breeze off the ocean.
Striped awnings and tents sheltered the many crafts-
people who had come from as far away as California
and Washington to sell their wares. A wide variety of
leather goods and jewelry as well as reproductions of
medieval weapons and costumes were for sale. Ven-
dors of meat pies and ale were making small fortunes
as the Revelers spent money with a lavish hand.

It was easy to distinguish the townsfolk from the
conventioneers. The locals were the ones dressed in
faded jeans, boots, tractor caps and Stetsons. They had
arrived in pickup trucks and four-wheel drives for the
most part. From the murmured comments, chuckles
and jokes Letty overheard, it was apparent that most
of the local people had come primarily to gawk and grin
at the strangers running around in outlandish costumes. The two groups did not mingle, but kept a certain distance from each other.

Letty paused for a few minutes to watch a wrestling
match and decided it was not her style of entertainment. She did not care if wrestling had been very popular in the Middle Ages. The sight of the sweating,
straining men reminded her too much of the fight that
Xavier and Sheldon had engaged in the previous evening. The memory brought back others of what had

followed. She moved quickly on to a puppet show that was taking place beneath a blue and white awning.

"Good morning, Letty." Alison Crane, her hand tucked under Richard Hodson's arm, smiled a cheery greeting. "Sir Richard, here, has asked to meet you. Richard, this is Letty Conroy, Sheldon Peabody's friend. Letty, meet the Lord of Revels and current Grand Master of the Order, Richard Hodson. The author. You've heard of him, I'm sure."

"I certainly have. In fact, I've read all your books." Letty extended her hand. She was mildly disconcerted when Hodson bent over her fingers and kissed them. "Oh." She hastily retrieved her hand.

"I am delighted to make your acquaintance, my dear." Hodson smiled with oily charm, his eyelids drooping in what he probably thought was a worldly, seductive gaze. "The Revelers are always eager to recruit members of your caliber. I am pleased you are attending our quarterly gathering as a guest."

"Thank you. I'm having a lovely time." Letty switched her smile to Alison. "I love that hat, Alison."

"Thank you, dear." Alison touched the brim of the open-crowned toque she was wearing over a veil. "I had it specially made from an old pattern I discovered in a book of medieval costume design. Turned out rather well, didn't it? Please excuse us. Richard, I believe we ought to be moving on. I see Judy Coswell over by the stage. I think I can talk her into giving me the listing on her condo."

"Yes, of course." Hodson gave Letty a lingering glance, eyelids drooping another quarter inch, mouth lifting at the corners with just the right touch of knowing intimacy. "We'll meet again, I'm sure, Lady Letitia."

Letty nodded and watched the pair as they drifted into the crowd. They she went toward a jewelry stall.

"Enjoying yourself, Letty?"

Letty spun around at the sound of Xavier's sardonic voice. He was not wearing a costume like the other Revelers, she noticed. Instead he had on a quietly expensive button-down shirt and a pair of dark, close-fitting trousers that had obviously been made to order. His hair gleamed in the sunlight and his eyes were very green. He looked a little dangerous, she thought. But, then, he always looked that way. He could not seem to help it. If Molly's suspicions were correct, he might very well be dreadfully dangerous.

But he had been so tender last night. . . .

"Hello, Xavier," she managed to say coolly. "I wondered where you were. I thought perhaps you'd gotten bored with all this fun and games business and decided to drive back to Tipton Cove."

"Not without you," he said. "I think it's time we had a talk, Letty."

"Honestly, you sound just like Sheldon. Why do so many people want to have serious talks with me lately?" She turned away to examine a gaudy necklace that sparkled on the table of the jeweler's stall. It was a cheaply made item, but it looked quite pretty in the sunlight.

"Peabody's been trying to talk to you, too? Figures. He's bent on finding a way to use you."

That annoyed Letty. "Has it occurred to you he might actually find me interesting and attractive?"

"He thinks he can get you to write a paper or a book with him and help him salvage his sagging career," Xavier said impatiently. "Don't be a fool, Letty. Steer clear of him."

"I'll tell you the same thing I told him. I can take care of myself."

"Uh-huh." Xavier leaned over her shoulder and picked up the necklace she had been studying. He examined it with a critical eye.

"You don't have to sound so skeptical. I'm an intelligent woman and I can take care of myself."

"Whatever you say."

"Xavier, let's get to the point. Are you going to explain why Molly can't turn up anything on you prior to ten years ago?"

He shrugged, still studying the necklace. "I changed my name. No big deal. It was a business decision. Nothing more."

"There's more to it than that, I can tell."

He slanted her an unreadable glance. "Can you?"

"Yes, but you're not going to tell me anything else, are you?"

"There's nothing else that you need to know. Besides, why should I make Molly's job any easier?" Xavier turned the necklace over and looked at the catch. "Are you thinking of buying this?"

"Yes, I was," Letty said.

"Don't bother. It's a piece of junk."

"It is not a piece of junk," she retorted, thoroughly incensed. "It's beautiful. I like it and if I decide to buy it, I will."

Xavier dropped the necklace back onto the velvet. "It's cheap and tacky and you know it. If you decide to buy it, it will only be because you're trying to prove to yourself that you don't need my advice."

He was right, damn him. "You know something, Xavier? I think Sheldon was right when he said you don't fight fair."

His eyes slid to hers. "I fight any way I have to in order to win. Remember that, Letty."

She stared mutely up at him and suddenly the day did not seem as warm and sunny as it had a few minutes earlier. There was a cold fire burning in Xavier's green eyes and Letty felt the now-familiar shiver flash down her spine. But it was not fear she felt. It was excitement.

Dangerous, she thought. *I know that. So why aren't I as frightened as I should be?*

"I don't like being threatened, Xavier," she said boldly.

"Neither do I."

"I haven't threatened you."

"Yes, you have," he countered. "You've threatened to end the engagement."

"That wasn't a threat, it was a promise," she shot back. "A vow. A fact. A fait accompli."

His eyes narrowed faintly as he studied her. "You're certain you want to call off the marriage?"

"Yes, I am," she insisted, knowing she was lying through her teeth. She was not at all certain what she wanted right now.

"Then why go to all the trouble of having Molly research my background?" Xavier asked softly.

"Revenge. Pure and simple. Besides, I've started an affair with you, remember?"

"How could I forget?"

For some reason his ready agreement on that point made her feel much better. He was not going to walk out of her life, after all, even if he was angry.

"In addition to sweet revenge," she told him, "I'm having you investigated because a woman in my position can't be too careful. If you turn out to be a mob boss or something, I want to know before the FBI knocks on my door."

"I see." Xavier took her arm and led her toward a stall where shortbread was being sold. "I've got a hypothetical question, Letty. If we were still planning on getting married, what would Molly have to turn up in her investigation to make you change your mind?"

Letty scowled up at him as he bought her a piece of shortbread. "What are you talking about?" She took a bite of the buttery cookie.

"I'm just asking you what sort of things in a man's background would make him unsuitable as a husband." Xavier munched his own shortbread, apparently not overly concerned with her response.

"Speaking hypothetically?"

"Of course. Our marriage has already been canceled according to you, so I'm just asking out of sheer masculine curiosity. What would a woman like you find unacceptable in a man's background?"

Letty considered that closely for the first time. When she had told Molly to carry out the search, she had not really stopped to think about what she might find.

"I don't know. I guess it would depend," she finally said honestly.

Xavier shot her a quick glance. "What the heck does that mean?"

"It means I don't know. It's hard to make judgments out of context, if you see what I mean. Of course, there are a few things that would certainly make me think twice."

"Such as?" he pressed.

"Well, if it turned out you had a half-dozen ex-wives running around, I'd be seriously concerned about your inability to make a meaningful commitment." She gave him a saucy smile, trying to lighten the atmosphere. "Or if you really are an ex-hit man or something along those lines, I'd be a little wary."

"So you don't approve of ex-wives or criminal records. Anything else?"

"Xavier, this is a ridiculous conversation."

"You started it when you told me you were having me checked out."

"I started it? What nonsense. *You* started this, Xavier." Letty came to a halt and swung around to confront him. "What about you? What sort of things in my past would have made you decide not to marry me?"

He gazed out over the throng of people milling around the brightly colored stalls. "It doesn't matter now, does it? The engagement is off, according to you."

"Damn it, Xavier, I want to know." Letty stepped closer and grasped a handful of his shirt in each hand. She stood on tiptoe and beetled her brow ferociously.

He was silent for a long moment as he looked down into her angry eyes. "A few months ago I could have given you an answer," he finally said quietly.

"I'm asking you right now. What would it have taken for you to decide I was unsuitable to be your wife?"

He shook his head slowly, his eyes steady and thoughtful. "I told you, I don't know. I can't think of anything you could have done in the past that would make me change my mind now about marrying you. Not now that I've gotten to know you."

Letty stood perfectly still, balancing herself on her tiptoes as she crushed the expensive fabric of Xavier's shirt. She stared into his unfathomable eyes. His answer unnerved her but she refused to admit it.

With a soft exclamation of dismay, she released him and stepped back. "Honestly, Xavier, I don't know what

to make of you. I just don't understand you at times,"
she muttered.

"I'm not so difficult to comprehend." He reached out
and caught her hand in his, lacing her fingers through
his own. "I'm just a man and I want you for my own.
What's so hard to understand about that?"

Letty struggled to stifle the warmth his words caused
to well up inside her. "The trouble with men is that
they're never as simple and straightforward as they
make themselves out to be."

"The trouble with women is that they can't resist
making things a lot more complicated than they really
are."

THE OFFICIAL INVITATION from the Lord of Revels to attend him in his suite arrived at Letty's door shortly before dinner. She scanned the brief note with a
considering frown. It was elegantly short.

My Dear Lady Letitia,
    As Grand Master of the Order of Medieval
Revelers and Lord of Revels, I hereby request that
you do me the honor of attending a small gathering in my suite at five this evening. Sherry will be
served and full membership in the Revelers will be
discussed.

Yours,
Richard

After a brief hesitation, Letty decided to attend the
small party before dinner. After all, she was here to
broaden her social horizons. In any event, she looked
forward to having an opportunity to talk to Richard
Hodson about his medieval mysteries.

She selected another colorful costume from the wardrobe and began to dress, aware of Xavier moving about in his room. She considered letting him know where she was going but told herself she should be more independent. She was sleeping with the man, but she was not married to him.

Letty just knew that if she gave Xavier an inch, he would take a mile. He was perfectly capable of commandeering the rights of a husband even if he was merely a lover. Something told her Xavier was the possessive type. She really should not get into the habit of always letting him know where she was going.

At five minutes after five, Letty arrived at Richard Hodson's suite. She listened for the sound of people within the room but there was no noise. Tentatively she raised her hand and knocked.

The door was opened immediately by Hodson. He looked very elegant in his gold and white surcoat and matching tasseled cap of soft white felt. The belt around his hips was a massive affair studded with imitation gems and ornate fittings.

"My dear Lady Letitia. How charming you look this evening. I'm delighted you could stop by for a glass of sherry." He smiled suavely down at her, his eyelids drooping with what was obviously intended to be rakish charm.

"Am I early?" Letty looked doubtfully past him into the suite and realized it was empty except for Hodson.

"Not at all, my dear, not at all. Right on time. Do come in." Sir Richard stood back from the door and beckoned her inside with a gracious gesture of his beringed hand.

"Thank you." Letty took a quick glance at one of the rings on his fingers and decided it looked like a real diamond. Apparently the medieval mysteries were paying well. Perhaps Sheldon was right in prodding her toward the non-academic market.

"A glass of sherry, my dear?" Richard went over to a tray containing a bottle and two small glasses.

"Yes, please." Letty glanced absently at the label on the sherry bottle and hid a small smile. She had been with Xavier when he shopped for sherry and she knew that particular label was one he disdained as cheap and bland. "Where is everyone else, Sir Richard?"

"I thought we would make this a private occasion, my dear." Hodson poured the sherry and handed her the glass with a small bow. "I wanted to meet you and talk to you alone, you see. I have a particular interest in encouraging you to join the Revelers. I have long admired your work in the field."

Letty relaxed. So this was going to be shoptalk—it was reassuring. "Thank you, Sir Richard." She wrinkled her nose thoughtfully as she tasted the sherry. It did taste rather bland.

He chuckled. "Just call me Richard. No need to stand on formalities. We are only playing games here at Greenslade, are we not?"

"Yes. But the games are rather fun." Letty smiled back at him as he drew her over to a sofa that faced the window. "Actually, I'm delighted to have an opportunity to talk to you. I don't want to sound like a gushy fan, but the plain truth is that I've thoroughly enjoyed all of your books."

"Have you? I'm honored." He sat down close beside her, his thigh brushing hers.

"I think you do a wonderful job with the research. Medieval history is obviously a passion of yours." Letty tried to edge her knee away from Hodson's but did not succeed.

"Passion is the perfect word for my interest in the medieval world," Richard said, sitting a little closer. "I find myself attracted to the period precisely because it was a time of high passion. Life was so much more vivid in those days. It was a world of extremes. The pageantry, the color, the warfare, the chivalric code and, yes, the great sexual liaisons. They were all taken to the limits of human emotions, enjoyed to the fullest by the people who lived then. Don't you agree?"

"Uh, yes." Letty took a quick sip of her sherry and tried to put some distance between her thigh and Richard's. "It was certainly a very colorful period. But quite brutal in many ways. And primitive. I mean, the sanitation standards were very low. Privies, chamber pots, garbage in the streets . . ."

"But for people like us, Letty, it was the ideal moment in history, I think." Richard struck an attitude of deep reflection. "It was a time that would have suited us admirably."

Letty coughed slightly and set down her unfinished sherry. "People like us?"

"People of intense passions," he explained. "I look at you, my dear, and I see a woman with a potential for truly great passion."

"You do?"

"Oh, yes, definitely." Richard edged closer. "Endless wellsprings of passion are buried in you, my dear. Oceans of passion. You were born out of time, just as I was, Letty. We belong to the age of Great Loves and High Passions."

"Excuse me, Richard," Letty cut in swiftly. "About my membership in the Revelers?"

"It is the duty of the Grand Master of the Order to personally interview and approve of all candidates. It is certainly my pleasure to carry out my duty in this instance. I think we have a great deal in common, my dear. And I know you will make a great contribution to the Order of Medieval Revelers."

"You do?" Letty asked doubtfully.

"Yes, I do." Hodson's arm slithered around her shoulders. "What's more, I believe you can make your contribution at the highest levels. You can serve as my personal assistant, Letty. How does that sound? Together you and I can transform the Revelers from a group of amateur medievalists to a dynamic organization of respected historians. Together we can lead the group into the future—help it achieve its full potential—gain academic acceptance of its accomplishments. Will you meet the challenge with me, my dear?"

"Uh—well, I've been giving the matter some thought and to tell you the truth, I haven't yet decided whether or not to become a full member. I'm certainly enjoying myself, you understand, but . . . oh, heavens. Just look at the time." Letty smiled brightly and leapt to her feet. "I've promised to meet someone. If you'll excuse me?"

"But, my dear, we have several things to discuss concerning your membership. We very much want to encourage people such as yourself who have academic credentials." Richard got to his feet and took her hand in his.

At that moment a sharp knock sounded on the door of the suite.

"Damn." Richard frowned. "Excuse me, Letty, while I take care of this. I left orders I was not to be disturbed."

He crossed the room and opened the door. "I thought I told everyone that I didn't want to be bothered before dinner. Oh, it's you, Augustine. What do you want?"

"Letty," Xavier said easily as he shouldered his way into the room. "I came to tell her we're going to be late for dinner. Ready to go, Letty?"

"Yes." She summoned up a smile that contained more relief than anything else. "I was just noticing the time. You will excuse us, Richard? Thank you so much for the sherry. I hope you'll autograph one of your books for me sometime."

"I'd be delighted." Richard gave Xavier a stiff smile, but his eyes were cold. "I don't believe anyone said anything about putting your name in for full membership, Augustine."

"Don't worry, I'm not applying. One of these conventions is enough for me. Let's go, Letty." Xavier dragged Letty out into the hall.

The door of the suite slammed shut behind them.

"I do believe," Letty said, "that I have just been entertained by what my mother would have called an aging roué."

"I found his note in your room. What the hell did you think you were doing going to his suite alone?"

"I thought there would be a crowd. It was supposed to be a pre-dinner cocktail party."

"Some party."

Letty started to giggle.

"What's so damned funny?" Xavier muttered.

"There was nothing to worry about," Letty said with a grin. "I wasn't in any danger. It was very cheap sherry. My standards have been considerably elevated since I met you, Xavier. Nowadays I would never allow myself to be seduced with a second-rate sherry."

MUCH LATER THAT EVENING Xavier opened the connecting door to Letty's room and walked in as if he owned the place. Letty, dressed in her prim, quilted robe, was standing in front of the closet, hovering over her selection of new nightgowns. She whirled around when she heard the door open and close behind her.

Xavier was wearing only a pair of black trousers. His broad shoulders gleamed in the bedside light. For a moment she simply stood there drinking in the sight of him.

"What's the matter, Letty?" He moved forward and lifted one of the wispy gowns out of her hands. "Can't make up your mind which one to wear for me?"

"I wasn't absolutely positive you'd show up here tonight," she admitted shyly.

"We're having an affair. Where else would I be at this hour?" He pulled her into his arms and covered her mouth with his own.

Letty sighed softly and wrapped her arms around his waist. His back felt sleek and strong and beautifully contoured. His masculine scent, tinged with soap and a recent shower, made her senses swim.

Xavier lifted his head and smiled as she melted against him. "Forget choosing a nightgown. You won't need one tonight."

He gently stripped off her robe and turned her so that she faced the full-length mirror that hung on the closet door. Letty gasped softly at the sight of herself standing naked in Xavier's arms. He slid his hands slowly down her sides to her hips and tugged her back against his thighs. He was hard with his arousal.

Xavier bent his head and kissed the curve of her shoulder. Letty leaned back against him, her knees suddenly weak. A fine trembling went through her. She knew Xavier felt it when she saw his slow, sexy smile in the mirror.

"Xavier?"

He cupped her breasts in his hands and nibbled gently on her earlobe. She felt his tongue on the inside of her ear and another shock of pleasure sizzled through her.

Then his hands were sliding down across the small curve of her stomach to the triangle of her hair below. Letty closed her eyes, her fingers clutching his forearms as she felt him part her softness. One long finger slid slowly into her and she cried out.

"You flow like warm honey." Xavier's voice was thick with desire.

"Please," she whispered.

"Yes." He wrapped one arm around her waist to hold her upright when she threatened to slide to the floor at his feet. With his other hand he probed her slowly and deliberately, finding the small, hidden bud and coaxing it into throbbing fullness. All the while he watched her in the mirror.

"Xavier." Letty caught her breath. Her fingers tightened around his arm. The tight, twisting sensation built. Letty grew frantic, wondering why he did not carry her over to the bed. "Xavier, the bed," she managed.

"Soon," he promised, his fingers still stroking, teasing and coaxing.

And then it was too late. Letty felt the great release and the pleasure that followed and cried out again. She lost what little remained of her strength and sagged against him with a soft moan.

"Oh, *Xavier.*"

"Now we'll try the bed," Xavier whispered as he picked her up in his arms and carried her across the room.

8

THE FOLLOWING EVENING the huge lobby of the Greenslade Inn was crowded as the night's festivities got underway. The musicians were getting warmed up and the Revelers made a colorful sight as they milled about in their spectacular costumes.

Letty noticed the spot of wine on her gown a moment after Alison Crane, who had paused to chat, swept off in search of a potential real estate client. Letty touched Xavier's arm.

"I'll just be a minute. I'm going down the hall to the ladies' room to sponge this wine out before it stains the gown. Be right back."

Xavier nodded and Letty headed for the door and stepped out into the hall.

The long skirt of her golden yellow gown swished lightly around her soft, pointed shoes as she walked quickly through the empty corridor. Behind her the muffled music from the ballroom filtered out into the hall.

She had left Xavier talking to a young amateur enthusiast who happened to be an expert on medieval warfare techniques. They had been deeply engrossed in a conversation about trebuchets and mobile assault towers, the terrifying engines of medieval warfare.

Letty pushed open the door of the women's room and thought about what was going to happen after the ball. A small rush of anticipation went through her as she admitted she was looking forward to Xavier's love-making.

And he was most definitely going to make love to her. She had no doubt at all about that. He had made his intentions very clear all evening long. Every time his glittering green gaze had caught hers, he had made his desire plain. He wanted her.

To think she had once questioned his virility. Letty grinned briefly to herself as she finished her business in the restroom and stepped back out into the hall.

"Oh, Letty, I've been looking for you." Alison Crane, dressed in a green gown and white cyclas and wearing a silver crespinette, came swiftly down the corridor. There were two more women behind her whom Letty did not know. They were both giggling. "There's something you simply must see."

"What is it, Alison?" But Letty was already being swept down the hall by the three costumed women. "Xavier will be expecting me back in the ballroom."

"This will only take a minute." Alison pushed open a door at the end of the hall and urged Letty out into the chilled night.

"Please, Alison, I really don't think—" Letty broke off as she saw the two knights waiting outside near a car. "What in the world is going on here?"

"Don't worry, Letty," Alison said reassuringly as the two knights swept deep bows and took hold of Letty's arms. "It's just a game. Part of the fun at the Revelers' conventions is initiating new members. Tonight your Xavier is going to prove his knightly valor by rescuing you. And just to make things interesting, he's going to have a little competition."

"No, wait, I don't want any part of this." Letty started struggling in earnest but she was vastly outnumbered.

Laughing, the knights and ladies bundled her into the backseat of the car and slid in beside her, locking the doors. One of the men got behind the wheel.

"Don't worry, Lady Letitia," one of the knights said cheerfully. "You're the prize in a quest. It's all part of the fun and games."

Letty turned her head to gaze helplessly back at the inn as the car drove off into the night. "Xavier is not going to like this," she warned.

"'Hear ye, hear ye,'" the man holding the scroll intoned following a dramatic drumroll and a couple of blasts on a horn. "'Sir Richard, the noble Grand Master of the Order of Medieval Revelers interrupts the revelry to announce a quest. All members of the Order will pay attention.'"

Shouts and applause broke out around the lobby and then an expectant silence descended as Sir Richard and his entourage made their way toward the dais.

"Sounds like something's up," the young man next to Xavier said.

Xavier gave up trying to learn more about the fire-power of medieval catapults and reluctantly turned to face the front of the room. He watched cynically as Richard Hodson, dressed in a heavily embroidered white surcoat, ascended the elevated platform and sat down in a heavily carved thronelike chair.

Xavier, wearing the black tunic with the gold leopard embroidered on it, decided he was getting bored with the endless games played by the Revelers. He wondered if he could talk Letty into leaving early. They could find their own private place on the coast, he thought as he glanced impatiently at his watch.

Where was Letty, anyway? Maybe there had been a long line in the ladies' room. Or perhaps she had run upstairs to her own room for something.

"My lords and ladies of the Order," Sir Richard said, speaking very solemnly into a microphone, "I fear we have a damsel in distress who must be rescued."

A cheer went up. Xavier frowned and glanced toward the door of the ballroom. There was still no sign of Letty.

"I wonder what this is all about," murmured the young authority on medieval war engines.

Sir Richard leaned toward the microphone as the cheers died down. "I have taken counsel with the members of the Inner Circle and we have reached a decision to send two bold knights on a quest to rescue the fair Lady Letitia from the clutches of the villains who hold her captive."

The crowd gave a roar of approval to this notion.

"*Letty.*" Xavier was suddenly paying full attention to what was taking place on the dais. "What the hell is going on here?"

"Sounds like you're about to find out," the young engineer observed.

Sir Richard held up a hand for silence. "We summon Sir Sheldon and Sir Xavier before us."

The engineer leaned closer to Xavier. "You'd better go up there if you want to find out what's happened to Letty. Sometimes the Order's idea of a game gets a little out of hand."

Xavier shot him a quick speculative glance and then turned and strode toward the front of the room. The crowd parted to allow him to pass.

"Go for it, Sir Xavier," a man called out. "My money's on you."

"He's too new at this kind of thing," someone else yelled. "No experience in quests. I'll bet on Sir Sheldon."

"I'll take Augustine," a woman declared. "Always stand on the side of the saints, I say."

Xavier ignored them all as he approached the dais. He saw that Sheldon Peabody was there ahead of him, resplendent in a short brocaded green satin tunic and a dapper little cap. He wore a flowing orange cape trimmed with elaborately scalloped edges. Xavier decided Peabody looked like some sort of comic book hero.

"What's this all about?" Xavier asked, making an effort to control his irritation. He came to a halt in front of Richard Hodson. "Where's Letty?"

"Ah," said Sir Richard with a knowing wink, "that is for one of you two stout knights to determine. A list of clues to her present whereabouts has been drawn up by the Inner Circle. The knight with the purest heart, the strongest sword and the most untarnished honor shall no doubt find her first. When he has rescued her from her captors, he will deliver her safely back here."

Sheldon gave Richard his most charming smile. "And is there any reward for the winner of this quest? Aside from the gratitude of the lady, that is?"

"Most definitely," Hodson said. "Whichever one of you returns with the fair damsel shall be rewarded not only with the lady's company for the evening, but with an honorary place among the valiant members of the Inner Circle for the duration of the year."

Another round of applause went up.

"Sounds good to me," Sheldon murmured, giving Xavier a sidelong glance.

Xavier ignored him. "This is stupid. Is Letty safe?"

"Quite safe. She is attended by three fair ladies and two of our most noble knights," Richard assured him. "And now the clues." He held out his hand with a regal gesture. Someone handed him two rolled-up scrolls. "Before you leave, you will kneel and make your solemn vow to strive to be successful in your quest."

Sheldon dropped dramatically to one knee, his cape swept back over his shoulders. "I vow to rescue the fair Lady Letitia and return her safely to this castle," he said in ringing tones.

Xavier gave him a disgusted look. Then he stepped forward and snatched one of the scrolls from Richard's hands. "Let me see that." He unrolled the paper swiftly and scanned the long list of obscure clues. "'A door of green,' 'a sea view,' 'an arrow's flight from the hamlet'? This is garbage."

"May the best man win," Sheldon drawled as he stood up and took the other scroll.

The last of Xavier's limited supply of patience finally evaporated. He looked at the Lord of Revelry. "I don't feel like playing your silly games, Hodson. I want Letty back here right now."

"Sorry, Sir Xavier. But the game is afoot and the only way to end it is to play it out and rescue your fair lady." Sir Richard chuckled jovially as he rose and started down the steps of the dais. "See you later."

Xavier watched Hodson make his way through the crowd for a moment, aware that Peabody was wearing a very satisfied smirk on his soft face.

"Well, well, well," Sheldon said. "Looks like you're going on a quest whether you like it or not. That is, of course, unless you'd rather let me go out alone to find the fair maiden. I imagine Letty would be a bit disappointed if you didn't show any interest in rescuing her but perhaps I can console her."

Xavier's gaze followed Richard Hodson's white tunic as it moved through the brightly garbed throng. "I don't play games, Peabody."

"You're playing this one." Sheldon chortled. "And you're going to lose. Now, if you'll excuse me, I'm going to start working on these clues."

Xavier did not bother to respond. Without a backward glance he headed into the crowd, making his way toward the doors at the far end of the room. Hodson had just disappeared through one.

Progress was slow because everyone wanted to give him an encouraging word or warn him that Sheldon Peabody was already getting the jump on him.

"Better get started, Sir Xavier. I'm afraid Sir Sheldon has the advantage. He's been on quests before," one man said as he clapped Xavier on the back.

"Thanks for the advice," Xavier muttered as he neared the doors.

"Good luck, Sir Xavier," a woman called out. "Remember, your lady's counting on you."

Xavier paid no attention to the well-wishers. He opened the ballroom door and stepped out into the wide corridor. When he glanced to the left he saw a white tunic disappearing around the corner at the end of the hall. Xavier followed. Sir Richard was headed for the castle privy.

The door of the men's room opened just as Xavier reached it. A balding, middle-aged knight came out. He was busy adjusting his tunic.

"Is it crowded in there?" Xavier asked easily.

"Nope. Just Sir Richard," the man said with a cheerful grin. "Plenty of room."

"Thanks."

Xavier walked into the white-tiled room. Hodson was standing at the sink, straightening the elaborate white and gold striped cap he was wearing. He glanced toward the entrance as Xavier entered.

"Hello, there, Augustine. Trust you're going to be a good sport about this," Hodson said smoothly. "Don't worry, it's all in fun."

"Sorry, I'm not going to be a good sport about it at all." Xavier grabbed the startled Hodson by the shoulder and slammed the man up against the tiled wall. He pinned him there. "Where's Letty?"

Alarm replaced the amusement in Hodson's astonished gaze. "Hey, what do you think you're doing, Augustine?"

"I asked you a question." Xavier drew back his fist.

"Hey, hold on a second, will you? It's just a damn game."

"What have you done with her?"

"Let me go. She's safe, I tell you."

"I'm not going to play your stupid game, Hodson. Nobody gets away with dragging Letty off into the night. Tell me where she is or I'll take you apart. Starting right now."

Hodson stared at him for a few seconds. What he saw in Xavier's eyes obviously made him decide that the game was over. "Look, it's no big deal, okay? Peabody wanted a quest that would pit the two of you against each other. The members of the Inner Circle thought it would be entertaining for the others so they agreed. We do it all the time. You two are both interested in Letty Conroy, so we made her the object of the quest. Simple."

"Did Letty agree to this?"

"Well, no, not exactly. She didn't know anything about it until Alison Crane and the others tricked her and got her into a car. Look, she's all right, I tell you. It's early. Nobody's started drinking. No one's in any danger."

"Where is she, Hodson?"

"You're supposed to follow the clues to find her," Hodson said, sounding desperate. "No, wait, don't get excited, I'll tell you," he added quickly as Xavier shifted his weight in preparation for the blow. "Damn it, man, you're serious, aren't you?"

"Yeah, Hodson. I'm serious. I don't like your games."

"Okay, okay. They've taken her to a little cottage on the other side of town. Take the main road along the ocean until you see a sign for Seaview Point. The house is on the right. It belongs to one of the Revelers."

"If you're lying to me, Hodson, I'll be back. And I'll be mad. Understand?"

"Yeah, yeah, I understand. What's the matter? Haven't you got any sense of humor?"

"Not much." Xavier released his victim and stepped back. "Remember, Hodson, if you've lied, I'll feed you your teeth."

Hodson straightened himself warily, shaking out his rumpled costume. "Hey, I believe you. What the hell am I supposed to tell Peabody?"

"I don't give a damn what you tell him as long as you don't tell him where she is. He likes quests. Let him follow those stupid clues."

Xavier was already at the door. A plump-looking knight dressed in green and pink entered just as Xavier went out.

"Say, there, Sir Xavier," the knight called out. "You'd better get going on your quest. Sir Sheldon just headed for the parking lot with a few of his buddies."

"I'm on my way."

"Good. My money's on you," the man yelled after him.

Xavier did not respond. He was striding down the hall, fishing for his car keys beneath the black tunic.

The Jaguar was right where he had left it in the parking lot, but it had been imprisoned. It was now barricaded behind a ring of other vehicles that had been strategically parked around it.

Obviously Peabody had taken his own approach to giving himself an edge in the quest. Several Revelers sat on the hoods of their cars, laughing and grinning as they waited to see what Xavier would do to rescue his besieged warhorse.

Xavier did not pause. It would take time to force several Revelers to move their cars. He ignored the hoots and shouts from the people sitting and leaning on the cars and walked toward an aging black Camaro that was parked on the outskirts of the steel ring. A man in a dark tunic and a woman with an elaborate headdress were lounging against the fender. They grinned at him as he approached.

"This your car?" Xavier asked casually.

"Yeah, it's mine," the man said. The woman beside him giggled. "What about it?"

"I think I'll borrow it."

The man straightened, alarmed. "Are you kidding?"

"You want to give me the keys or would you rather I hot-wired it?" Xavier was already reaching for the door handle.

"Now just a damned second here. You can't take my car."

"Watch me." Xavier slid into the front seat and bent down, seeking under the dash with knowing fingers. It had been a few years since he'd tried this. He'd have to trust that the old feel was still in the fingers.

The owner of the car leapt forward with a strangled yelp, obviously recognizing expertise when he saw it. "Wait, don't start ripping up my wiring, for crying out loud. Here, take the damn keys."

"Thanks. I appreciate it." Xavier caught the keys as they were hurled at him. He slammed them into the ignition and put the Camaro in gear.

"Well, hell," the Camaro's owner breathed as Xavier spun the wheel and sent the vehicle racing out of the parking lot. "This is going to be interesting." He rounded on a friend who was watching curiously. "Hey, Sam, let's follow Augustine."

Xavier heard a few enthusiastic shouts behind him as he drove out onto the main road, but he did not bother to glance back. He was in a hurry.

LETTY SAT in the corner of the old sofa, her knees drawn up under the skirts of her gown and stared glumly at the checkerboard. "I wish you would listen to me, Alison. Trust me, this is not a good idea. Xavier is going to be very annoyed."

"Relax, it's a game. Everyone has a good time and we all party afterward." Alison sat back from the checkerboard. "Your move."

Letty reluctantly pushed a piece on the board. The rest of the group who had spirited her away into the night were munching potato chips while they watched television and made bets on how long it would take for Peabody to show up.

"Afraid Sheldon will probably be the winner," one of the men had confided as he dumped more chips into a bowl. "He's been on quests before and he knows how to follow clues. It's sort of like a scavenger hunt. Augustine ever been on one?"

"I doubt it," Letty had said. She could not imagine Xavier Augustine going on a scavenger hunt. "He's not the type."

She was not exactly a prisoner in the beachside cottage, Letty knew. She had already made one trip to the bathroom to scout out the situation and had discovered there was nothing to prevent her climbing through the window.

The problem was what to do after she was out of the cottage. The night was cold, rain was on the way and she did not have a coat with her. Letty was quite sure none of the others would give her the keys to the car so her only option was walking all the way into town, a distance of perhaps three or four miles. The road back to town would be a long and lonely one.

In a true emergency she would have risked the hike, of course. But given the fact that she was in danger of Xavier's uncertain temper, she had decided not to try to escape. She would just have to wait for her *verray, parfit gentil* knight to show up.

"Nice little cottage, isn't it?" Alison said in a chatty tone as she made another move on the checkerboard. "One of my clients owns it. It was a steal. Estate sale, you know."

"It's very pleasant." Letty hesitated, wondering how much of an advantage Sheldon's previous experience on quests would give him. "Alison, I wish you'd listen to me. Xavier is not into this kind of thing. He's going to be worried about me and he will definitely not be in a good mood when he gets here."

One of the men sitting in front of the TV glanced over his shoulder. "Don't worry, we'll explain it all to him. Just a game. All the new members have to go through a quest or something. Revelers have a reputation to uphold. If you want to be a member in good standing, you've got to know how to have fun."

Letty shook her head. "I don't think Xavier wants to be a member in good standing."

"Then he can get lost," the other man, whose name was Carl, said lazily.

"Don't be a spoilsport, Letty." Alison jumped two of Letty's men and crowned a king for herself. "Let's talk about something else."

"Like what?"

"How about that book I was telling you to write?"

"I'll think about it." Letty shifted a bit on the couch and strained to hear the noise of an approaching car. She thought she could hear a distant roar but knew it was probably the sound of the ocean. "It's kind of isolated around here, isn't it?"

"That's the beauty of the place," Alison assured her. She picked up a checker, started to put it down and then paused, tilting her head attentively to one side. "Hey, everyone, I think I hear a car."

Letty leapt to her feet. The distant roar she had heard was a vehicle after all. But it did not sound like the sophisticated purr of Xavier's Jaguar, she realized, disappointed. She hurried to the window. "Someone's coming. More than one car."

"Maybe Augustine and Peabody are neck and neck," Carl said as he joined her at the window. "Get ready to be rescued, Letty."

"What the heck?" The other knight peered out the window into the darkness. "There's a whole bunch of cars coming this way. What's going on?"

"Do you suppose a few of the Revelers decided to follow the two knights on their quest?" Alison asked.

"I don't know." Carl frowned. "I'm not sure I like the looks of this. They're arriving too soon. There hasn't been time for the two knights to figure out the clues. And there are some pickup trucks in that group of cars following the Camaro."

"Pickup trucks?" One of the other women who had accompanied them leaned closer to the window and frowned. "I don't think I remember any pickups being parked in the lot at the Greenslade Inn. Where did those come from? What in the world is happening out there?"

"I'm not sure, but they're definitely coming this way." Carl edged back from the window, digging out his keys. "You know, it might not be a bad idea if we got in the car. This is making me a little nervous."

"Wait a second, I recognize that black Camaro in the lead. That's Bob Frazer's car, isn't it?"

"Maybe. Maybe not. This is turning weird."

"Why would Frazer be leading the rest of them? He's not a member of the Inner Circle and he's not on the quest. How would he know where we went with Letty?"

Everyone turned to stare accusingly at Letty, who shrugged her shoulders. "Don't look at me. Xavier doesn't play by other people's rules."

"Hell, let's get moving." Carl was already leading the way outside.

The others, including Letty, followed quickly into the cold night.

The black car in the lead was pulling into the drive, its headlights sweeping across the small group of people hurrying toward Carl's car.

The Camaro came to a shuddering halt and the driver's door was thrown open. Xavier, looking exactly like what he was supposed to be in his black attire—a medieval knight bent on rescue and retribution—leapt out.

"Letty, over here. Hurry." He ran toward her.

Letty turned at the sound of his voice. *"Xavier."* She picked up her skirts and dashed toward him.

He caught her up in a grip of steel and bundled her into the front seat of the Camaro.

Carl yelled at him over the top of his own car. "Augustine? Is that you? What's going on?"

"I picked up a few camp followers. Some of them are friendly but I don't know about a few of the others. They're from town. You know how it is, everyone loves a parade." Xavier was already behind the wheel of the Camaro, shoving it into gear. "If you want my advice you'll get the hell out of here."

"Damn." Carl jumped into his car and his friends piled in after him.

Xavier gunned the Camaro's engine and roared out of the drive. Carl was close behind.

Letty turned in the seat and stared out the window at the line of cars angling off the main road into the cottage drive. Horns were sounding, tires were screeching, music blared from car speakers and people were yelling. It was quite a sight.

"You always do things first-class, don't you, Augustine?" she murmured as she leaned back and fastened her seat belt. "I have never been rescued before, so I can't speak from personal experience. But something tells me this little scene is going to pass into legend in the chronicles of the Order of Medieval Revelers."

"Unfortunately, it isn't over yet." Xavier pressed his booted foot down harder on the accelerator. "We still have to go back through town. Bound to pick up a few more followers. This time the cops are likely to notice."

"Oh, my." Letty fell silent as she envisioned the size of the thundering horde that would be arriving back at the Greenslade Inn. "Xavier, this is getting a little out of hand. What are we going to do when we get back to the inn?"

"You are going to follow orders." Xavier checked his rearview mirror. "We've got a few minutes' lead. They're all still milling around back at the cottage, trying to figure out where the action is. Except for the idiots who kidnapped you. They're right behind us."

"It wasn't exactly kidnapping and they're not idiots, Xavier. Just an overzealous group of fun-loving history enthusiasts."

"They're idiots. And it was kidnapping as far as I was concerned. You didn't go with them willingly, did you?"

"Well, no. I didn't want to go, but it was a little hard to refuse, if you know what I mean. They were very insistent." Letty sighed. "I told them you weren't going to like it."

"You were right. I hope you've had a good time during the past three days, Letty, because it's all over now."

She shot him an uneasy glance. "What do you mean?"

"I have a hunch the quarterly meeting of the Order of Medieval Revelers is about to come to an unexpected conclusion. With any luck at all, we'll miss the fireworks. Now, listen up, Lady Letitia. When we get back to the inn, I'm going to park at the rear entrance. You and I are heading straight upstairs to our rooms. We're going to pack all our things in five minutes flat and then we're going to get in our cars and drive straight home to Tipton Cove."

Letty's eyes widened. "All the way back to Tipton Cove? Tonight? Xavier, it's after midnight. I don't feel like a two-hour drive."

"You'd better get in the mood, because that's what you're going to do."

"But why?"

"Because I have a hunch the Revelers are going to make a few headlines tomorrow morning and I don't want you showing up in the news photos."

"News photos." Letty was aghast. "Xavier, what do you think is going to happen?"

Xavier glanced into the rearview mirror again, his mouth grim. "When that crowd behind us roars back through town a second time and picks up a police escort, there will be hell to pay. There's already some tension between the locals and the Revelers. Didn't you notice it yesterday at the fair? We're going to be safely back in Tipton Cove when the big raid gets plastered across the front pages."

"Oh." Letty digested that. Then she sat back in the seat and smiled to herself.

Xavier shot her a sidelong glance. "What are you thinking about now, Letty?"

"I was just thinking that it's all been quite exciting. In the past three days I've broken off an engagement,

I've had two men do battle over me, I've started an affair, I've been the intended victim of a seduction by an aging roué, I've been the object of a quest, I've been rescued by a knight riding a black destrier and now I'm in danger of figuring in a scandalous newspaper story."

"Yeah, I see what you mean," Xavier said coolly. "I guess it doesn't get any better than this, does it?"

"Go ahead and be sarcastic if you want," Letty said, folding her arms under her breasts. "But I'm telling you this is the most excitement I've had in my entire life."

He threw her a burning look. "Tell me something. Out of all the exciting things you've done this weekend, which was your favorite?"

"Oh, that's easy. Starting the affair."

Xavier was silent for a long moment and then he grinned slowly, a very wicked, male grin that spoke volumes. "What a coincidence. That was the thing I liked best, myself."

Letty smiled in the darkness. "You know something, Xavier?"

"What?"

"I knew you'd rescue me. I never doubted it for a moment."

"Is that right?"

"Uh-huh. I don't know what you did before you materialized as Xavier Augustine ten years ago, but whatever it was, you must have been good at it. I can't wait until Molly finds out just who and what you were before you became a saint."

"Letty?"

"Hmm?"

"This is not a good time to bring up the subject of the investigation you and Molly are trying to conduct into my past. I am not feeling indulgent."

"Right. Whatever you say, Xavier." Letty started to laugh and then she spotted a familiar car passing them, going the opposite direction. "Oh, look. There goes Sheldon."

"He must have finally figured out the clues Lord Richard gave him."

Letty's brows came together in a thoughtful expression. "Everyone kept saying Sheldon had the advantage because he'd been on quests before and knew how to decipher the clues. How did you manage to get to the cottage ahead of him? And why are you driving this car instead of the Jag?"

"I don't always play by the rules."

Letty smiled with satisfaction. "That's just what I told Alison."

9

"Letty? Letty, honey, wake up."

"Not time to get up," Letty mumbled into the pillow. "We just got into bed."

"It's five-thirty. Up and at 'em." Xavier leaned over the bed, pulled back the covers and gave Letty an affectionate slap on her rear.

"Five-thirty?" She forced open her eyes and turned to peer resentfully up at Xavier. Even without her glasses she could tell he looked far too vigorous considering the circumstances. He was dressed in sweats and a pair of very expensive, very high tech running shoes. "We didn't get in until late last night. Why do we have to get up now?"

Letty had been drooping with weariness when she finally pulled into the drive of her little Victorian house in Tipton Cove last night. Even as she had opened the car door, the lights of Xavier's Jaguar had swung into the narrow lane behind her. He had followed her closely all the way from the Greenslade Inn.

They had barely made it out of the inn's parking lot as the first of the parade of cars had begun returning. The vehicles that had chased after Xavier on the outward bound trip had been supplemented by several more pickup trucks and a smattering of four-wheel drives on the return trip.

Letty, driving away from the inn at a discreet speed, had heard the first of the police sirens in the distance.

Xavier had been right, she had reflected as she reached out to turn on the radio. Things were about to get even more lively at the quarterly convention of the Order of Medieval Revelers.

She had experienced a brief moment of regret at being obliged to miss the excitement that was bound to ensue, but staying around to participate was out of the question. A glance in her rearview mirror had revealed Xavier's Jaguar already hard on her tail, herding her forward on the long drive home.

When they reached Letty's house, both she and Xavier had literally fallen into bed and gone straight to sleep.

"Letty," Xavier said again, disturbing her memories of how she came to be in her own bed this morning, "you have to get up now. I'm not joking."

"Give me one good reason."

"All right, I will. You have to get up so you can go for an early morning run in the park."

"Running? You want to go running? After all that dashing around last night? You're out of your mind." Letty shoved her face back into the pillow.

Xavier swore softly under his breath. "Letty, pay attention. You have to go for an early morning run so that by noon everyone in Tipton Cove will know that you were right where you should have been when the big raid at the Greenslade Inn took place."

That comment finally succeeded in riveting Letty's attention. She sat straight up in bed, clutching the sheet. "What raid?"

"The one that netted our esteemed Lord of Revelry and a certain member of the local Tipton College academic community." Xavier handed her the *Tipton Cove*

Herald, the town's slender morning paper. Then he held out her glasses.

Letty put on the glasses and looked down at the front page of the newspaper. The *Herald* generally featured extensive coverage of such titillating topics as the fate of the latest sewer bond issue or Tipton College's recent academic appointments. But this morning it had a much juicier story to report. "Celebrity Author and Tipton College Prof Key Figures in Fracas."

"'Fracas'?" Letty looked up. "Is that what they call it?"

"I believe fracas is a professional journalistic term meaning something along the lines of a barroom brawl."

"Oh." Letty stared down at the headline for a long while. Beneath it was a photo of Richard Hodson and Sheldon Peabody being assisted into the back of a police cruiser. They were still wearing their medieval attire. The expression on his florid face made it clear Hodson was trying to explain just how famous he was. The policeman did not look impressed. Perhaps he did not read medieval mysteries.

Sheldon, on the other hand, was trying desperately to conceal his face with the hem of his tunic. He hadn't succeeded.

The lights of the Greenslade Inn blazed in the distance, revealing the entire, sordid scene. A throng of knights and ladies could be seen standing on the lawn behind the police car. They were apparently engaged in exchanging insults with a crowd of local farmers and cowboys. Beneath the photo was a caption.

Well-known author Richard Hodson and Tipton history prof taken into custody during an alter-

cation between townsfolk and convention goers at Greenslade Inn. No charges were filed and the pair was later released.

"Oh, my goodness." Letty dropped the paper on the bed and raised her eyes back to Xavier's cooly amused gaze.

"My point, precisely," Xavier said. "Our goal this morning is to show everyone that you were nowhere near the Greenslade Inn when the 'altercation' occurred." He tossed her a red long-sleeved sweatshirt and matching pants. "Move, honey."

"What if I don't mind everyone knowing I might have been involved in something like that?"

"I mind." Xavier bent down and yanked her flannel nightie off over her head. He stood gazing down at her breasts for a moment, looking regretful. "And while there are other things I would rather do this morning than go for run in the park—" he touched one nipple and watched with appreciation as it went taut "—I must be strong for your sake."

"But we're not going to get married, so my reputation or lack of it, doesn't matter any more." Vividly aware of her nipples puckering in response to his touch and the look in his eyes, Letty grabbed the sweatshirt and put it on. Then she reached for the pants.

Xavier threw her a thoroughly disgusted look as he went to the closet to find her running shoes. "What about your career, Letty? You want Stirling to think you were mixed up in that raid?"

"I don't care what he thinks," she said defiantly as she put on the scuffed and worn shoes.

"Easy to say now. You'll feel differently when you've had a chance to think about it."

"Oh, yeah? Says who?"

Xavier handed her a brush. "Says me."

"Why are you still trying to protect my reputation? We're merely involved in an affair now. It's okay to have affairs with fast women, you know." She got up, went into the bathroom and yanked the brush through her hair.

Xavier's mouth kicked up at the corner as he watched her. "I don't have affairs with fast women," he said gently.

"What kind do you have them with? Slow women?"

"Don't get sassy."

She closed the door on his wicked grin. "What is this, Xavier?" she called out as she ran water in the sink. "You're so upright and proper that even your mistresses have to be above reproach?"

"You're really looking for an argument this morning, aren't you? Yesterday morning wasn't much better, as I recall. I think I'm beginning to see a pattern here. Are you always this hostile when you wake up?"

"Sometimes I'm worse," she assured him as she walked back out into the bedroom.

"I'll keep that in mind. Come on, I don't have time to spar with you now." He grabbed her hand and hauled Letty firmly toward the front door.

"Do we have to go through this?"

"Stop whining. It's for your own good."

"You mean it's for your own good," she sniped, feeling distinctly peevish as she stepped out into the crisp morning air. "I don't think I'm up to running. How about a nice, leisurely morning walk?"

"You have to look fit and robust. Can't have anyone thinking you might be hungover or otherwise suffering from your three days of orgies and debauchery."

"Such a lovely word, debauchery. You know, Xavier, I don't feel that I really had a chance to experience much debauchery at Greenslade. I was just starting to get the hang of it when you made me leave." Letty allowed herself to be urged down the front steps and along the path to the garden gate.

"You've had plenty of excitement lately. What about the brawl? What about beginning an affair? What about getting kidnapped? Wild times in the fast lane, if you ask me." Xavier unlocked the front gate.

"I'm not saying that what there was of it wasn't exciting."

"I suppose I should be grateful for that much," Xavier muttered as he closed the gate.

Letty frowned thoughtfully. "You know, Xavier, it occurs to me that you caused most of the excitement I did get to experience."

"Me?" He gave her a reproachful glance as they started past Dr. Knapthorpe's rosebushes.

"Yes, you." Letty warmed to her topic. "You were the one who actually started that brawl. You were the one I had the affair with. You were the one who caused that fracas at Greenslade by refusing to play the quest game by the rules."

"I'm hurt."

"Hah. You know something else? I'm beginning to suspect you're something of a fraud, Xavier. You're not the saint you pretend to be, are you?"

"I never pretended to be a saint. Just a man who prefers a nice, peaceful existence. I don't think that's too much to ask out of life. Morning, Knapthorpe." Xavier raised a hand in greeting as Professor Knapthorpe, dressed in a bathrobe, came out onto his porch and waved.

"Good morning, Augustine. Letty." Knapthorpe nodded genially. "Thought I heard you two come in last night. Missed all the excitement down the coast, I see." He indicated the headlines on the *Tipton Cove Herald* he was holding.

"We left the convention early," Xavier explained, leaning casually against the white picket fence. "It wasn't quite what we had expected. Letty and I realized shortly after we got there that it really wasn't our kind of thing."

"I should say not." Knapthorpe shook his head and tut-tutted. "Peabody certainly seems to have made a fool of himself. Can't think what Stirling will have to say about this."

"A very unfortunate incident," Xavier said, looking grave.

"Yes, isn't it? You two certainly showed good sense leaving the convention early. But, then, that's only what I would expect of you both. Neither one of you is the type to involve yourself in a messy situation like this nonsense down the coast."

"No, sir," Xavier agreed. "Letty and I much prefer the quiet life, don't we, Letty?"

Letty gave him a saccharine-sweet smile. "Our muscles are going to tighten up in this cold air if we don't get moving."

"Right you are," Xavier said cheerfully. "Can't have tight muscles. Off we go. See you later, Professor."

"Certainly." Knapthorpe nodded in a friendly fashion and turned toward his front door. He paused briefly and glanced over his shoulder. "How are the wedding plans coming?"

"Invitations are going out this week," Xavier said before Letty could open her mouth.

"Excellent. I'm looking forward to it."

"That reminds me," Xavier said. "Letty has no one to give her away. We were wondering if you'd do the honors?"

"Xavier." Letty's voice was a high-pitched squeak of dismay.

Knapthorpe looked vastly pleased. He beamed at Letty. "Why, I would be happy to do so. Very kind of you to ask. Never done that sort of thing before. Never had any daughters of my own. It will be a delightful experience. I shall look forward to it."

"It's settled then. See you, Professor." Xavier took Letty by the arm and urged her off at a slow trot.

Letty was still recovering from the shock. She had never been so incensed. "Xavier, how many times do I have to tell you, the wedding is off? How dare you go and ask Knapthorpe to give me away? What am I supposed to say when he finds out the truth?"

"We'll worry about that later. Right now the important thing is to make everyone think things are perfectly normal. Run, lady."

"Please, Xavier, I can barely move, let alone run."

"I told you, this is for your own good."

Letty sighed deeply and managed to move from a slow trot to a jogging run as they headed around the block to the park.

As with many college towns, Tipton Cove was filled with fitness enthusiasts and on any given morning one could count on the park to be filled with runners, joggers and people walking briskly along its shaded paths. This morning was no exception. Letty and Xavier passed at least ten people by the time they reached the pond at the far end. Each person they saw seemed surprised and somewhat relieved to see them.

"Morning, Letty. Morning Augustine. Glad to see you didn't get mixed up in that mess down the coast."

"Hi, you two. I see you're back early. Good thing. Hear it got a little hairy at that convention of medievalists."

"Hey, I didn't realize you two were here in Tipton Cove. Thought you'd gone off down the coast. Just as well. Word has it Peabody got himself arrested at that convention. Can you believe it?"

"Letty. Augustine. Glad you're back in town. Heard there was a big riot at Greenslade. Good thing you weren't involved."

Letty groaned as Xavier prodded her along the second lap of the park course. "Talk about being the focus of all eyes. I get the feeling everyone in town knows we went to that convention and they all seem to know what happened last night."

"Told you so."

"Please, Xavier. Not at this hour of the morning. I'm barely surviving this marathon as it is. I don't need you telling me you told me so."

"Sorry."

"You don't sound sorry in the least." She shot him a glowering look, aware that he was moving easily without any apparent effort beside her, deliberately slowing his pace to match hers. He was not even breathing hard. "How can you run around like this after a night like the one we just had?"

"Fear is a great motivator."

"Fear of what people will say about me if they don't see us out here?"

"Exactly. Tell you what, I'll buy you a nice fresh cinnamon roll at the Park Street Café," Xavier said. "How does that sound?"

"Assuming I make it as far as the Park Street Café, it sounds all right," she allowed grudgingly.

"Bound to be a crowd in the café by this time," Xavier noted, glancing at his watch.

"I get it. More witnesses to the fact that we're here in Tipton Cove instead of languishing in jail."

"You're catching on fast."

The first person Letty spotted when Xavier opened the door of the Park Street Café a short time later was Dr. Elliott Stirling, chairman of the Tipton College history department. The professor was paying the cashier for the cup of coffee he had just finished consuming.

Stirling glanced up expectantly when Letty and Xavier walked into the cozy restaurant. He frowned slightly into the morning sunlight behind them and then his noble brow cleared as he recognized his bright, young medieval studies scholar and her fiancé. He nodded his patrician head in regal acknowledgment of their presence.

"Dr. Conroy. What a surprise. Heard you'd gone down the coast to attend that convention of amateur medieval history buffs."

Xavier smiled blandly at Stirling as he escorted Letty to a nearby table. "Letty and I gave it a whirl but decided to come back early when we realized it wasn't a genuine, academically oriented convention."

"Quite." Stirling gave Letty an approving look. "I wouldn't have said it was your sort of thing, Dr. Conroy. Glad to see you had the sense to leave early. Too bad certain other members of the department didn't demonstrate the same degree of intelligence." Stirling nodded once more and then went out the door.

"Poor Sheldon." Letty sighed and picked up her menu.

"As far as I'm concerned, he got what he deserved," Xavier said.

"How can you say that?"

"He was trying to use you, Letty. I told you that."

"I wish you'd stop saying that," she muttered.

"I'm saying it because it's the truth. You want one cinnamon roll or two?"

"One."

"I'll order two for you. That way I can eat the extra one." Xavier closed the menu and smiled at the waitress. "Two cinnamon rolls for the lady and I'll have two, also. And two cups of coffee."

"Right. You two see the morning paper?" the young waitress inquired with a bright-eyed expression.

"I glanced at the headlines on the way out the door this morning," Xavier admitted.

"Really weird about Professor Peabody, wasn't it? I had him in History 205 last quarter. It seems strange to have a professor do something stupid like that. Be right back with your orders."

Letty glared across the table at Xavier. "I hadn't realized just how little privacy there is around this town."

"Told you so."

"Say that one more time, Augustine, and I'm going to cram my napkin down your throat. I didn't ask you to rescue me, you know."

"It was my pleasure."

Letty sighed. "I guess, now that I think about it, it's a good thing I'm here this morning and not in the headlines along with poor Sheldon."

Xavier grinned, looking pleased with himself. "You know, Letty, this would be a very good time for you to start wearing your engagement ring again."

She eyed him suspiciously. "Why?"

"Because it will help stifle speculation and gossip. You don't want them talking about you the way they're going to be talking about Peabody. Don't worry, you can always take it off again in a few days after all the fuss has died down."

"I don't know, Xavier, it seems sort of dishonest."

"Think of it as protective camouflage." Xavier had already reached into his pocket and pulled out the ring. He took her hand gently in his and slid the emerald back into place. "There, that should help quell some of the comments."

Letty gazed sadly down at the emerald. It winked back at her in the sunlight. "Well, all right. If you're really that worried about what people will say, Xavier."

"Thank you, Letty. I appreciate it."

There was more than humble gratitude in his tone, Letty thought. There was also one heck of a lot of cool, masculine satisfaction.

THE RED LIGHT was glowing on Letty's telephone answering machine when she and Xavier walked back into the house an hour later.

"You go ahead and take a shower," Letty said to Xavier. "I'll listen to my messages."

"Fine."

There had apparently been several calls. Letty pushed the playback button and heard Molly Sweet's anxious voice.

"Letty? Where are you? I tried the inn but they said you'd checked out in the middle of the night. What's going on? I have to talk to you."

The second message was in a similar vein but there was no doubt but that the anxiety level had escalated in Molly's voice.

"Letty? Call me as soon as you hear this. I have to talk to you. Things are getting sticky."

The third call sounded even more urgent. "Letty, I'm not kidding. This is serious. I must talk to you ASAP. It concerns you-know-who. Call me. Oh, damn. Where are you?"

Letty frowned in growing concern as the last of the anxious messages concluded. She sat pondering the situation for a moment, listening to the sound of the shower going in the bathroom. Then she picked up the phone and dialed Molly's home number. Her call was answered midway through the first ring.

"Letty? Is that you?"

"It's me, Molly. What's happening?"

"I don't know." Molly sounded extremely agitated. "But I'm afraid I may have gotten all of us into some very deep water. I have to talk to you. Someplace private. Don't bring Xavier, whatever you do."

"Why can't I bring Xavier? Does this have something to do with your computer search?"

"Yes. I've been getting more of those strange inquiries from some source that won't identify itself. They're getting spooky, Letty."

"Threatening inquiries?" Letty's fingers tightened around the phone.

"Veiled threats, if you know what I mean," Molly said in an ominous tone. "Letty, this could be dangerous."

"Dangerous? To whom? Xavier?"

"Maybe. Or maybe to us. I just don't know. Look, I'm afraid to say anything more over the phone."

"Oh, my God. You think whoever's sending those threatening inquiries over the computer might have tapped your phone, too?"

"I just don't know. We can't take any chances. Meet me at the pond in the park. That's out in the open so it should be reasonably safe. Ten minutes."

"I'll be there." Letty replaced the phone, wondering what sort of excuse she could give to Xavier for dashing back out of the house. She suddenly realized the shower had gone off while she had been talking to Molly.

"Any important messages?" Xavier asked casually from the hallway.

"Oh, no." Letty jumped and swung around to see him fastening his trousers and stuffing his shirttail into his waistband. She wondered if he had overheard anything. He did not sound curious or suspicious. She cleared her throat. "That is, no important messages. Just Molly trying to get in touch with me. Xavier, I've just realized I'm out of milk. I'm going to run down to the convenience store on the corner and get some. Be right back."

His brows rose. "I thought you were exhausted from our early morning run."

"Yes, well, I've recovered. Women recover from exercise much faster than men, you know. Scientific fact. And I won't actually be running to the store. Just sort of sauntering along." Letty pinned a bright smile on her face and edged toward the door. "Be right back." She let herself out the door and closed it firmly behind her.

Xavier crossed the parlor and looked out the window. Letty was running, not sauntering back toward the park. He wondered when she would realize she had not taken her purse.

Xavier went over to the phone and dialed Hawk's number.

"What's going on, Hawk?" Xavier drawled when the phone was picked up on the other end. "Threatening inquiries? Phone taps?"

"Maybe a few of the former but definitely none of the latter, although it might prove interesting." Hawk was totally unperturbed. "I'd like to hear Molly Sweet's voice. The lady is sounding more and more interesting by the hour. How's it going on your end?"

"You've got Molly and Letty agitated as hell. What have you been doing?"

"I've been blocking all of Ms. Sweet's data base queries. I'm letting her think she's getting into forbidden territory. Implied she was asking for top secret information and asked to see her clearances. She keeps backing out and trying from new directions. Very clever, our Ms. Sweet. I'm having fun. Want me to keep up the good work?"

Xavier leaned back in the chair, propped his feet on the ottoman and stared thoughtfully out the window. "Yeah, I think so. Stall for a while longer."

"Still having problems with your lady, huh?"

"My lady thinks she's into excitement these days. And she's decided having an affair with me is a lot more exciting than getting married to me."

"She's calling off the wedding?"

"The wedding is still on," Xavier informed him roughly. "She just doesn't know it."

"Still not ready to tell her about your past?"

Xavier's mouth tightened. "No."

"Sounds like you've made up your mind and once you do that, you're like a rock. I won't even try to change it for you." Hawk chuckled. "I'll just go back to playing games with Ms. Molly Sweet. What's she look like?"

"Who? Letty?"

"No, not Letty. Molly."

"Oh." Xavier frowned, trying to think. "Wears glasses. Got kind of a bizarre taste in clothing. She's about Letty's age." He floundered, unable to think of any other salient characteristics. "Smart. Sort of attractive, I guess."

"Married?"

"No." Xavier suddenly realized where this was leading. "You sound like you're interested."

"I like her persistence," Hawk said. "She's gutsy."

"Just keep her out of my past," Xavier muttered. "At least until I figure out how to salvage my future."

"I'll do my best. Good luck." Hawk hung up the phone.

LETTY SAT on the park bench beside Molly and stared at the ducks on the pond. "This is beginning to make me very nervous."

"Tell me about it." Molly, dressed in a fuchsia and electric blue striped top over tight black leotards, scowled behind her glasses. "But I've saved the worst until last. I think he knows where I am, Letty. I think he even knows my name."

"What?" Letty was horrified. "Are you certain?"

Molly nodded grimly. "He started making little jokes on the computer. Wordplays on my last name. The inquiries all start with some dippy salutation like, 'Hi, sweetcakes' or 'You again, sweetheart?' This morning it was 'What do you want this time sweets?' He knows my last name is Sweet, Letty. And if he knows that much, he knows too much."

"I see what you mean. That does sound suspicious."

"I think I'd better stop the search, Letty. I don't know what I've opened up here."

"I think you're right." Letty stood up abruptly. "I'm going to have a talk with Xavier. This has gone far enough. I am going to demand some answers."

"Be careful, Letty." Molly got to her feet, looking worried. "The more I think about this, the more I'm afraid we may be in big trouble."

"I'll call you as soon as I talk to Xavier. I'm going to tell him what's happened and tell him I need to know if you're in any danger."

"I'm going straight home," Molly said. "I'll wait for your call."

Letty nodded and broke into a run. She was certainly getting her exercise this morning, she reflected bleakly.

She arrived back at her house a few minutes later, pushed open the garden gate, dashed up the porch steps and threw open the front door. The aroma of hot coffee drifted down the hall from the kitchen.

"Xavier?"

"In here," he called from the kitchen. "Get the milk?"

"Forget the milk. We have to talk." Letty hurried down the hall and came to a halt in the kitchen doorway. Xavier was fiddling with the coffee machine. "Xavier, I have something to tell you. Something serious. And I need some answers."

He hesitated and then turned around slowly to face her. He looked a little dangerous and a little wary. "What is it you have to tell me?"

Letty drew a deep breath. "I told you I asked Molly to make some inquiries about you."

"So you did." He folded his arms across his chest, his eyes never leaving her face.

Letty chewed her lip. "The thing is, someone seems to have discovered that she's asking questions."

"And?"

"And Molly is afraid we may have opened up a very big can of worms," Letty concluded in a rush. "She thinks whoever discovered she was prowling around in the computer data bases now knows who she is and maybe even where she lives. Xavier, you have to tell me the truth. Is Molly in any danger because of the way she's been probing your background?"

Xavier blinked, as if that was not quite the question he had been expecting. "No," he said slowly. "There's no reason for Molly to be in any danger."

"Are you absolutely certain?" Letty pleaded.

"Absolutely certain. Molly's in no danger."

A rush of relief went through Letty, emboldening her. "Then I think it's time you leveled with me, Xavier."

His eyes glittered. "What do you want to know?" he asked a little too softly.

"Isn't it obvious? I want to know if you're the one who's in danger."

He looked blank for a moment. "Depends on how you define danger, I guess."

"Xavier," she yelped, "don't pussyfoot around the issue. Does this have something to do with a . . . a legal problem in your past?"

"That's a tactful way of putting it. Look, Letty, I think I . . ."

"It's all right. You don't have to explain everything now. Just tell me this much—would it be awkward for you if people found out about your past?"

"Yes," Xavier said.

"I knew it. Oh, God, you are in danger." She hurled herself across the kitchen and into his arms, burying her face against his very expensive shirt. "And it's all my fault."

His arms closed fiercely around her. "Honey, it's all right."

"No, it isn't all right. If I hadn't told Molly to conduct that search none of this would have happened. Oh, Xavier, I'm so sorry. I never meant to put you in danger. I was just trying to get a little revenge because you had me investigated. Please forgive me."

He kissed the top of her head. "I forgive you."

She raised frightened eyes to search his face. "Do you swear it?"

"I swear it." He smiled slightly. "Word of honor."

"And Molly's safe?"

"Perfectly safe."

Letty stepped back. "Then we have to get out of here. Now. Before he comes looking for you."

"Before who comes looking?" Xavier asked curiously.

"The person who's tracking Molly in the computer. Don't you see? Whoever he is, he already knows too much. He's figured out that Xavier Augustine is you. By searching for your past, Molly's accidentally tipped him off that you're still around. What's more, she's afraid he now knows where she lives. Which means he can figure out where you are."

"This is getting confusing, Letty."

She grasped his shoulders and tried to shake him. It was like trying to shake Mount Everest. "Don't you see? Xavier, whoever it is you've been hiding from for the past ten years now knows where you are. We have to get out of here right now. We can't afford to waste another minute."

"Where are we going?"

"Into hiding, of course. We're going to lie low until the heat dies down."

10

"I CAN'T TALK long. Letty went out to pick up dinner. She'll be back soon." Xavier paced back and forth in front of the motel room window, his eye on the parking lot. It was filled with eighteen-wheel trucks, pickups, and a variety of aging Chevvies and Fords. There wasn't a BMW, Mercedes or Jaguar in sight. Across the street a garish neon sign signaled a fast-food restaurant.

"What the hell is going on?" Hawk demanded.

"I told you, we're on the lam. Hiding out. Living on the run. Heading for the border."

"The Mexican border?"

"No, not yet. Right now we're heading for the California border. But at the rate things are going, we may be on the way to Mexico next. Or Canada. I'm not sure. This is Letty's operation. She's saving me, you see. At the moment we're holed up for the night in a cheap motel off the Interstate."

"A *cheap* motel?" Hawk laughed. "That doesn't sound like you, Augustine. You always go first-class."

Xavier spotted Letty hurrying across the parking lot with a white paper bag in her hand. She had the collar of her windbreaker pulled up high around her ears and she was casting suspicious glances over her shoulder. He grinned. "I told you, Letty is managing this escape and she thinks we'll be more inconspicuous in a budget motel."

"Isn't having a Jaguar parked outside the room going to look a little strange?"

"We left the Jag hidden in Molly's garage. We're driving Letty's little compact. Look, she's coming back to the room now so I've got to hang up. Just wanted to let you know what was happening."

"A thrill a minute," Hawk said dryly. "You want me to keep up the pressure on Molly Sweet?"

"Yeah. For a while longer. Letty says we have to stay out of sight until Molly gives the all clear. Molly says she'll do that when she's convinced that whoever's backtracking me through her computer has given up."

"Right. I get it. I'm the bad guy. Guess I'll go play the role of unseen computer menace," Hawk said. "Hey, Augustine?"

"Yeah?"

"You know something, old buddy? You sound like you're actually having fun."

"I am."

"Looks like you've got all the proof you need now that the lady isn't about to ditch you because of your sordid past."

"Funny how things turn out. I never planned it this way, but that's what happened. It feels good, Hawk."

"Well, good luck on your run for the border."

"They'll never take me alive," Xavier vowed. "Talk to you later, Hawk." He put down the phone as Letty inserted her room key into the lock. Then he went to open the door.

"Everything okay?" Letty asked as she shot one more glance back over her shoulder and quickly slipped into the room. She turned to throw the bolt.

"No problem." Xavier smiled at her as he took the paper bag from her hands. She was breathless and disheveled and there was a scattering of raindrops on her jacket. Her hair had long since slipped its moorings and chestnut tendrils floated around her shoulders. "Nobody around out there except a few truckers pulling in for the night. What did you bring us?"

"Fish and chips from the fast-food place across the street. Oh, and I got a bottle of wine from the convenience store next door and some plastic glasses." Letty looked at him uncertainly. "It's just a jug wine, I'm afraid. Nothing special. They didn't have much of a selection."

Xavier pulled the screw-cap bottle of generic red out of the bag and did not even wince at the sight of the cheap label. "I need a glass of this. You serve dinner, honey, and I'll pour the wine."

"Okay." Looking relieved, Letty set about unwrapping the contents of the paper bag. The aroma of fried fish and chips filled the small room. "I know this isn't quite what you're accustomed to, Xavier, but I figure no one will look for you in a place like this."

"You're probably right." Xavier hid a rueful smile as he glanced around the tacky little motel room, noting its faded drapes, sagging bed and worn shag carpeting. The television was chained to the wall. "It's a great place to hide out."

"I just wish we knew how long we'll have to lie low." Letty's brows snapped together over the frames of her glasses as she sat down at the small table.

"I don't think we'll be on the run for long," Xavier said, thinking of the wedding invitations waiting to be addressed and mailed. "Not for more than a few days at the most."

"You think whoever Molly alerted will give up that quickly?"

"Probably. I don't think he's the persistent type. Just doing a routine check." Xavier poured the wine into two disposable cups.

"I'm not so sure about that. He seems to be taunting Molly. She was very nervous."

Serves her right, Xavier thought wryly. "Trust me. Molly is safe." Xavier took a swallow of the red. "You know, this stuff isn't all that bad."

"What? The wine? Oh, good." Letty tried hers. "Tastes like the kind they serve at the pizza parlor in Tipton Cove."

"The perfect accompaniment for fast food," Xavier declared, taking another taste. "Did you bring any catsup?"

"It's in the bag." Letty gave him a narrow glance. "You know, something, Xavier?"

"What's that?"

"You don't seem quite as worried about what's happening as you should be."

"You have to be philosophical about this kind of thing, Letty. A survivor learns to roll with the punches."

"When are you going to tell me what it was you survived ten years ago?" she asked softly.

Xavier plunged a French fry into the catsup. "It's a little hard to talk about after all these years."

She reached across the table to touch his hand. "Don't you think I ought to know what we're facing?"

"Maybe. But I haven't talked about this with anyone for ten years, Letty."

"I understand. Don't worry, I'm not going to push you." Letty withdrew her hand and picked up a plastic fork. "I can see you don't feel comfortable in confiding in me yet. But I hope you will one of these days."

He exhaled heavily. "Soon, Letty. Soon. I promise."

The fish and chips and cheap red wine served up on a rickety table in a budget highway motel room proved to be one of the finest meals Xavier had ever enjoyed. He knew he would treasure the memory for the rest of his life and he knew why. He was beginning to believe that Letty could love him in spite of his past.

When he had asked her to marry him, Xavier had been confident that Letty had fallen genuinely in love with the man he was today. She had fallen for the very successful and eminently respectable Xavier Augustine, a man who endowed college faculty chairs; a man who knew the difference between real French champagne and California sparkling wine; a man who always traveled first-class.

But now Xavier allowed himself to wonder if maybe, just maybe, Letty could love the man he had once been.

"I'll take the remains outside and dump them in the garbage bin," Xavier said when the last of the fish and chips had disappeared. "Otherwise this room will smell of fried fish all night."

"Be careful," Letty said, looking anxious again.

He kissed the tip of her nose. "Relax. No one's going to see me."

He bundled up the wrappers and let himself out into the damp night. The smell of rain was in the air, making everything seem fresh and new. Xavier found himself whistling as he walked over to the garbage bin. On the way back to the room, he glanced up and saw the moon winking down at him through scuttling clouds.

Life, Xavier decided as he let himself back into the cheap little motel room, looked very good tonight.

Letty was just emerging from the bathroom, wrapped in her prim, quilted robe and wearing a pair of fluffy slippers. Her hair was loosely pinned on top of her head and her face was freshly scrubbed. She pushed her little round glasses higher on her nose and smiled tentatively at him.

It occurred to Xavier that she was feeling somewhat shy. He smiled back at her as he closed and locked the door. "The thing about affairs," he said gently, "is that one is usually obliged to conduct them in hotel and motels rooms. Which is what we've done so far, isn't it?"

"You're an authority?" she asked tartly.

He shook his head as he started unbuttoning his shirt. His eyes never left hers. "No. But I've heard tales."

Letty sat down on the edge of the bed, clutching the lapels of her robe. "Well, I don't imagine it would be much different if we were married," she said briskly. "We'd still be on the run and still forced to stay in places like this."

"Somehow," he said as he sat down beside her and unlaced his shoes, "I think things would be a lot different if we were married."

"Why?"

"Just a feeling." He let his shoes drop to the floor and sat beside her, his shirt hanging open. He gazed thoughtfully at the darkened TV set across the room. "Letty?"

"Yes?"

"There's something I'd like to know."

She stirred slightly. "What's that?"

"Well, I was just wondering if an affair is all you're ever going to want from me."

"Xavier..."

"I mean, now that you've turned over a new leaf and you're into excitement and adventure, maybe you're going to get bored with me as soon as the heat is off and we're no longer on the run."

Her eyes widened. "Xavier, how can you say that? I can't imagine ever getting bored with you. Even when you were playing the part of the perfect gentleman, I was never, ever bored. Frustrated at times, but definitely not bored."

"Yes, but you're a new woman now. You might not feel that way when our lives return to normal. If I went back to my old life, you might decide to go out and find someone more exciting."

"Stop saying things like that."

"I don't know, Letty." He got up slowly, went across the room and switched off the overhead light. The neon light from the fast-food restaurant sign made the curtains glow a dull orange. "I've been thinking it over and I'm not sure I want to go on like this."

In the dim orange glare filtering through the drapes he could see the sudden alarm on her face.

"Like what? You don't want to go on having an affair?"

He shook his head as he sat back down beside her. Then he leaned forward and rested his elbows on his thighs, his hands clasped loosely between his knees. "It's the uncertainty, you see. I don't think I can handle it. I've already got too much uncertainty in my life as it is."

"You do?"

"I'm afraid so. There's the basic uncertainty of my business, of course. People in my line of work are always at financial risk. And then there's the uncertainty of not knowing when or how my past might catch up with me. That's a constant concern, especially at the moment. It all adds up to a lot of pressure. I'm not sure

I can handle the added uncertainty of having an affair with you."

"I hadn't thought about it quite like that. Was that why you had me investigated, Xavier? Because you were trying to eliminate some of the uncertainty in a relationship?"

"In a way. Do you think you can ever forgive me for that, Letty?"

Her fingers tightened on the lapels of her robe. "I suppose I'll have to after what I've done."

"Don't blame yourself for what happened when you started digging around in my past. You couldn't have known."

"True," she agreed. "To tell you the truth, I expected your past to be as dull as my own."

"I never considered your past dull. Not for a minute."

"That's because you wanted a woman without a past," she reminded him grimly.

"I just wanted to know what I was getting into." He turned his head to look at her. "But it wouldn't have mattered what I found. I'd still have wanted to marry you."

Her eyes searched his. "You say that now when you know there's nothing in my background to cause you any problems. But what would you have said when you first got the report if the investigation had shown some major scandal in my past?"

"There's nothing I can say or do now to prove that I would have married you anyway. But doesn't it mean anything to you to know that I still want to marry you, even though you're into the fast life these days?"

"Well . . ."

"Letty, do you still love me a little?"

She threw her arms around him. "Xavier, I still love you a lot," she whispered against his chest. "I've never stopped loving you."

"You're not just saying that because I've gotten more exciting lately?"

"No, I swear it. I do love you, Xavier. I love the old you and the new you."

"I wish I could be sure of that," he said, stroking her slender back with gentle hands. "Things have gotten so mixed up lately."

"Xavier, I promise you there is nothing uncertain about my feelings for you."

"You're sure?"

"Absolutely sure. What do I have to do to prove it, for heaven's sake?"

"Say you'll marry me. Even though we're on the run."

"Yes, damn it," she said, sounding thoroughly exasperated, "I'll marry you. Now, please stop trying to talk about it. I'm the one who's getting confused."

She pushed him abruptly down onto the bed and kissed him with a fierceness that took away Xavier's breath. He felt an overwhelming urge to laugh in soft, loving triumph but there was no opportunity. Letty was all over him, raining kisses across his mouth and his throat. Xavier's rush of satisfaction turned into flaring desire.

"*Letty.* Ah, sweetheart, that feels so good."

Her small, delicate fingers trailed across his chest, sliding under his shirt to find the flat nipples hidden in the crisp, curly hair. Her tongue touched his skin and Xavier groaned.

He felt as if he were being attacked by a horde of butterflies. It was a wonderful sensation. Within seconds he was hard with need. He started to unknot the sash of Letty's robe.

"Xavier, I do love you so. Please believe me."

"I believe you." He had her robe open now. Underneath it she wore a transparent peach-colored nightgown. Xavier knew he was looking at another one of the new gowns she had purchased for her trousseau.

Even as he started to ease the robe off her shoulders, Letty was busily at work on his belt. He obligingly lifted his hips when she started awkwardly pushing his trousers and briefs down over his thighs. At last he was wearing only the unbuttoned white shirt. He felt himself throb when her fingertips touched him intimately. Xavier breathed deeply, fighting to control the raging need. His blood ran hot.

"Damn, Letty. You don't know what you do to me."

"I'm glad you want me," she whispered. "For a while I wasn't sure that you did."

"You know better now, don't you?" he growled. He managed to get her robe off at last. Then he shifted position so that he was lying full-length on the bed. He pulled her down on top of him. The skirts of the peach-colored gown swirled around his hard body. "Show me how much you love me, sweetheart." He caught her face between his hands, dragged her mouth down to his and kissed her deeply. "Show me how much you want me."

"Yes. Yes, my love."

She kissed him back with frantic eagerness, her hands touching him everywhere. There was an endearing, sweet wildness in her lovemaking as she struggled to please him.

Xavier gloried in the waterfall of feminine sensuality that was pouring over him. He felt the weightless nightgown glide along the inside of his leg, teasing and tantalizing him. Letty's hips ground against his. Her bare foot slid along his calf. Her tongue plunged daringly into his mouth.

Xavier was vaguely aware of the harsh glare of the orange neon sign illuminating the bed. From time to time a whiff of frying hamburgers found its way into the room. There was a dull, distant roar of engine noise from the traffic passing by out on the Interstate. Somewhere a trucker leaned on his horn. A television blared next door.

None of it mattered. The only thing that mattered was the scent and taste and feel of the woman in Xavier's arms. She loved him.

He reached down and pulled the hem of the peach gown up over Letty's sweetly shaped buttocks, all the way to her waist. Then he caught hold of her silken thighs and parted them until she was sitting astride him.

Bracing herself with her palms flattened against his chest, Letty gasped and looked down at him.

"Xavier?"

He smiled, reached up and plucked off her glasses and set them down on the dresser beside the bed. Then he slid his hands slowly up along the insides of her legs to where the womanly wet heat awaited him. When he found her slowly with his fingers she closed her eyes and shuddered. Her reaction electrified all his senses.

"Letty, you make me feel like the most powerful man on the face of the earth." He lifted her slightly away from him and then eased her down onto his heavily engorged manhood. The gossamer fabric of the nightgown foamed around his thighs and drifted across his flat stomach.

Xavier urged her gently downward, filling her slowly and surely with himself.

Letty sucked in her breath as she adjusted to him. Xavier luxuriated in the sensations ripping through him. He had to set his teeth to keep from rushing the climax.

"You feel so good," he muttered, his voice hoarse and rasping with sexual tension. "So good." He lifted his hips experimentally. He could feel her clinging all along the length of his shaft. His head whirled.

"Oh, Xavier, *please.*"

"Yes," he said through his teeth. "*Yes.*"

He guided her into the rhythm and she responded with everything that was in her. Xavier closed his eyes as he surged into her again and again.

She cried out softly and trembled in his grasp. He opened his eyes to watch the play of emotion across her expressive face as she found her release. Xavier thought he had never seen anything so glorious in his life. She loved him even though she thought he was on the run from a past he could not tell her about.

She loved all of him, past and present.

He felt the last of her gentle, rippling climax begin to fade and then he let himself go, driving himself deeply into her one last time. His guttural, half-stifled shout blended with the sounds from outside.

Xavier tightened his arms around Letty and held her close against his sweat-dampened chest as she collapsed against him. When he opened his eyes a while later he found himself staring up at the patterns created by the orange neon glow on the ceiling.

He thought he could see his future and his past in those patterns. And for the first time, they were joined together in a way that at last felt right.

LETTY STIRRED beneath the covers, instinctively exploring with one big toe for Xavier's muscled leg. She frowned into the pillow when she did not discover it.

That was when she realized she could hear him talking somewhere. She turned amid the sheets and yawned.

"Xavier?"

"Over here, honey. Just a second."

She opened her eyes and saw that he was sitting at the small table, talking into the phone. He was dressed only in his trousers, his chest bare. His hair was still rumpled from sleep. He gave her a quick, intimate smile and then went back to his conversation.

"That's right, it's all over, Hawk. Leave poor Molly in peace. And don't forget, we'll be expecting you at the wedding." Xavier paused, listening. "Damn right, it's going to be formal. And since you're going to be best man, you'd better start shopping for a tux. What? . . . You better believe it. First-class, all the way. So long. I'll talk to you later." He hung up the phone.

Letty struggled to assimilate the meaning of the mysterious conversation. "Hawk? As in Hawkbridge Investigations? Xavier, what's going on here?"

Xavier leaned back in the chair, legs wide apart and ate her up with his eyes. "Don't move. I'm coming right back to bed in a minute but first I just want to look at you."

She held up a hand. "Hold it right there, Augustine. What was that call all about? Hawkbridge Investigations is the firm you hired to run that background check on me. Any connections to the person on the phone?"

"Yes."

"Well? Why are you talking to that outfit again? Why did you tell whoever it was that we're going to have a formal wedding?"

"Because we are. Just as I planned all along. The man I was talking to is a friend of mine. The best one I've got. His name is Hawkbridge but everyone calls him Hawk."

"You said something about leaving Molly alone. He's the one who's been terrorizing her on the computer?"

"He was just trying to stall her while I sorted things out on this end." Xavier smiled with satisfaction. "But we've got everything sorted out now, don't we?"

Letty scowled as a vague suspicion rose in her mind. "Xavier, are you playing some kind of game with me?"

"Not exactly. Well, maybe. In a way. It's a little difficult to explain, Letty. But I'm going to try over breakfast."

She reached for her glasses and put them on. Her intuition told her something was very wrong here. "You will explain now, please."

He grinned lazily. "I'd rather wait. I've got more interesting things to do at the moment." He stood up and started to unsnap the fastening of his trousers.

Letty tensed. "Sit down, please. I want the explanation now, Xavier. I don't like this feeling that something's been going on behind my back."

He studied her briefly, amusement still edging his hard mouth. "What the hell. Why not? Might as well get it over and done." He sat down again, one arm resting casually on the table. He rubbed his jaw thoughtfully. "This is a little complicated."

"Don't worry about the complexity," she retorted. "I'm quite bright."

He grinned. "That's right, you are, aren't you? Ph.D. and everything."

"Is it so difficult to remember?" she asked very sweetly. "Perhaps you keep forgetting because I have this nasty habit of making a fool out of myself around you?"

"Whoa. Take it easy, honey. I never said that."

"Tell me why you were on the phone first thing this morning to that man named Hawk."

"I told you why. I'm calling him off the case. I no longer need him to stall Molly." Xavier leaned forward, his eyes growing serious. "It's a long story, Letty, but I'll try to keep it short because it's not a very interesting story."

"Suppose you start with who you really are."

"I really am Xavier Augustine."

"Legally?"

"Very legally. I told you, I changed my name ten years ago. Perfectly legal."

She stared at him. "Why?"

He sighed. "Because my life was a mess, my career was in ruins and my fiancée, who had played me for a chump, had just run off with the man I had been working for. On top of that, I had come very close to taking the rap in a case of fraud. I damn near went to jail, Letty. My reputation was in shreds. There was no way I could salvage it. So I walked away from my past and started fresh under a new name."

"My God."

"Yeah." His smile turned wry. "Hawk was a friend. The only one I had left when it was all over. He runs a firm that handles investigations and security matters for business. He knows how to pull apart someone's past. That means he also knows how to construct a new one."

"And he did that for you?"

"He helped me build up a new identity after I changed my name. He also set up some computer traps and triggers in certain major data banks used for credit checks so that he'd get a warning if anyone ever started prying to closely into my background. Having someone discover the truth about my past could have seriously jeopardized my new business relationships. Once you've been tainted in a fraud case, it's impossible to convince clients you're clean."

"So he was alerted when Molly started checking on you?"

Xavier nodded. "Right away. He called me while we were at the Revelers' convention and asked me what I wanted to do. When I realized you were behind the check, I told him to stall. I didn't want you finding out about my background at that stage."

"You were afraid I wouldn't approve? Is that it? Xavier, how could you think that?"

"You have to look at this from my point of view," he said patiently. "You're a classy lady."

"Oh, for pity's sake . . ."

"It's true. You've got it, honey. The real thing. Not flash and glitz, the kind of class anyone can buy, but *real* class. You're a lady in the old-fashioned sense of the word. You come from a whole different world than the one I hail from. You've got a fine education, a clean, respectable past, a good reputation. You've got the respect and admiration of others in your field. And on top of everything, you're very nice."

"Nice?" Letty was appalled. "That's all you can find to say about me? I'm *nice?*"

Xavier paused, obviously searching for the right words. "You're kind to people. A good friend. People trust you. You're honorable. You've got integrity."

"I sound like a Boy Scout," Letty said in disgust. "I keep telling you I'm not that virtuous," she snapped. "Never mind. Keep talking."

Irritation flashed in his glance. "You know what your problem is? You take it for granted."

"Take what for granted?"

"Your good name. The respect people have for you. The whole bit. You've always had it, so you assume it's the norm. But it wasn't. Not for me, at any rate." He ran a hand through his hair. "Damn. There were times when I wanted respect so badly I could taste it. I would have paid any price for it."

"What are you trying to say?" Letty asked quietly.

"I was born on what they used to call the wrong side of the tracks. My parents split up when I was three years old. I never saw my old man again after he left. My mother waited tables to support me. I started getting into trouble the day I realized people judged her by her clothes and her background and the kind of car we drove. It was my way of fighting back. I wouldn't let anyone get away with treating her like dirt."

"Oh, Xavier..."

"I was into one scrape after another at school and had a couple of brushes with the law. Then my mother died in my senior year of high school and I dropped out. I never even finished high school, Letty."

"You're self-educated. So what?"

"That's only the beginning," he told her. "The worst is yet to come. I finally landed a job in the mail room of a small investment firm in Southern California. I worked my tail off to get noticed and within six months I was out of the mail room and working as an assistant in one of the offices. After that there was no stopping me. Once on board, I didn't waste time. I had a flair for that kind of thing. I learned fast and I was willing to work twenty-four hours a day. The boss was a red-hot entrepreneurial type. He didn't care about anything except the bottom line and I always delivered."

"So you moved up fast?"

"Very fast. The money started rolling in. I'd never seen so much money in my whole life. And along with the money came respect and that was even better. People knew I was successful and they admired me for it. It was a heady thing, Letty. For the first time in my life, I was making it."

"What went wrong?"

"Along with the money and the respect came a very beautiful, very sophisticated woman named Constance Malton. I'd ever seen anything like her. She was the perfect Southern California dream made flesh. She knew more about life in the fast lane than you could ever hope to learn, Letty, even if you devoted your whole life to the project. Hell, I think she was born in the fast lane, although I sure didn't realize it at the time."

Letty bristled. "I see."

Xavier smiled indulgently. "Believe me, honey, you aren't the type. Hell, your idea of fast living is to run off to a convention of history buffs and get yourself kidnapped by a bunch of folks wearing medieval costumes."

Letty felt suddenly extremely naive. "You must have found it awfully amusing when I told you I intended to become a more exciting sort of woman."

"No, Letty, I was not amused. I was angry with myself for having made you think you had to change, though."

"What happened to your Southern California dream girl?"

"We were going to get married. Had it all planned. Just as soon as my boss concluded a monster land deal he was working on. In the meantime I had to handle the office." Xavier's eyes hardened. "He pulled it off, all right. And as soon as my boss had stashed the money in a Swiss bank, he and my fiancée left for foreign climes. The government walked into my office before I'd even realized I'd been set up to take the fall."

"It was an illegal deal?"

"It was a very complicated piece of fraud. A scam. I was set up by my fiancée and my boss to look guilty. Some wealthy, powerful people got taken and when the smoke cleared, I was the only one left around to prosecute. I was innocent. I'd had no idea of what was going on with the land deal. But before it was all over I spent everything I had on lawyers trying to clear myself. I managed to do it. Then I found it didn't really matter. Everyone still thought I was guilty."

"You couldn't shake the stigma of having been connected to the fraud, is that it?"

Xavier nodded. "That's it. The fact that I was found innocent of all charges didn't seem to mean anything. My business reputation had been shot to hell."

"So you started over."

"With Hawk's help," Xavier agreed. "He also helped me finish things."

"What does that mean?"

Xavier paused a beat and then said deliberately, "I finally figured out a way to bait a trap for Constance and my ex-boss. I needed Hawk's expertise. He helped me put the plan together, helped me pull it off. We lured them back to the States with a deal that was too good to be true. They fell for the setup and the Feds were waiting."

Letty shivered at the ice in his voice. "So you got your revenge on them."

"Did you think I'd let them get away with what they had done?" Xavier asked softly.

"No," Letty said. Xavier would have been implacable in his vengeance. Just like any medieval knight in shining armor. She turned that over in her mind for a minute. "Why did you feel you had to run an investigation on me?"

Xavier exhaled slowly. "If I'd had the sense to check Constance Malton out earlier on, I would have discovered that she was a professional conartist. She'd lured more than one male to his financial doom. I was very young and desperate to prove I could succeed. That made me easy pickings for her. After Constance, I swore I would never let another woman set me up for a fall."

Letty pondered the tale. "So what it basically comes down to is you had to be certain I wasn't another Constance Malton before you asked me to marry you."

"Can you blame me?" Xavier asked softly.

That did it. Letty leapt off the bed and grabbed her robe. "Yes, damn you, Xavier Augustine, or whatever your name is. I do blame you." She raced around the small room, stuffing her things into her suitcase. "You've made a fool of me right from the start. You don't love me, you love my pristine reputation and my naiveté. You've manipulated me for the past few days. You even tricked me into thinking you were in danger from something that had happened in your past."

"Letty, honey. . ." he began soothingly.

"When I think of how you must have laughed to yourself yesterday after I told you I was going to go into hiding with you, I could scream." She yanked on her jeans and grabbed a shirt. Then she stepped into her loafers.

"Letty, are we going to go through this scene again?" Xavier asked coldly. "Because if so, you might as well know I'm tired of it. This has gone far enough."

"I agree completely." She headed for the door, suitcase in hand.

"Letty, come back here." He realized belatedly that she was actually going to leave. He got up and went to the door as she opened it and went out. "I said, come back here."

"Forget it."

"What do you think you're doing?" he yelled after her. "You told me you loved me, by God."

"I do." She opened the car door and threw her suitcase inside. Then she slid into the front seat. "The old Letty would have forgiven you instantly, taken pity on your traumatized past and thrown herself into your arms. But this is the new Letty and I've had it with being sweet and understanding."

"Come back here."

"Pay attention, Xavier Augustine. Until you decide you love me, *me*, not my virtuous past or my stalwart integrity or my respectable academic reputation, you can forget any idea of marrying me or of having an affair with me." She turned the key in the ignition.

"Listen to me, honey."

"I don't feel like listening to you. You're not saying anything I want to hear. Do you know you've never once told me you loved me? Not once." She shoved the gear lever into reverse and stamped her foot down on the pedal.

The car roared out of the parking lot.

Xavier stood in the doorway for a long time after the little car had disappeared. Then he turned back into the room and packed up his belongings.

When he was ready he walked out to the road that led to the northbound on-ramp and stuck out his thumb. Fifteen minutes passed before a big rig slowed to a halt. Xavier recognized it as one that had spent the night in the motel parking lot alongside Letty's car.

The trucker watched as Xavier opened the door and climbed up into the cab. "That your little gal I saw leaving like a bat out of hell a few minutes ago?"

"Yeah. Thanks for stopping."

"Sure." The trucker shook his head as he cranked the eighteen-wheeler onto the Interstate and headed north toward Portland. "Got yourself a little domestic crisis, I take it?"

"Uh-huh."

"Sorry to hear that. She important to you?"

"More important than she knows," Xavier said. "But it looks like I haven't done a very good job of telling her."

The trucker nodded sympathetically. "The thing about women is that they like to hear the words, you know?"

"I gave her plenty of words but they weren't the right ones."

The trucker shot him a curious glance. "You got 'em straight now?"

"Yeah. I've got 'em straight now."

11

LETTY GAZED MOROSELY down at the anchovy and onion pizza that occupied the center of the table. "I shouldn't have done it, Molly. I was an idiot to do it. It was too big a risk. He'll never come after me now. He has too much pride. I shouldn't have pushed him that far."

"Why did you?" Molly helped herself to a slice of pizza.

Letty sighed. "Finding out he'd let me make a fool of myself by thinking I was saving him from his past was, well, it was the last straw. He doesn't love me, Molly. Not really."

"I wouldn't be too sure of that."

"No, it's the truth. I have to face facts. He was making me prove myself again, just as he did when he had me investigated. He enjoyed watching me try to rescue him. I tell you, Molly, I'm sick and tired of proving my love for Xavier Augustine. He can damn well prove his love for me this time around."

"How's he going to do that?"

"By apologizing and telling me he loves me. Do you realize he's never actually said it?" Letty shook crushed hot peppers on the pizza. "Not once, damn it."

"You'd believe him if he did say it?" Molly asked curiously.

Letty was astounded at the question. "Of course. Xavier would never make a commitment like that unless he meant it."

"I see. Well, he's been awfully persistent for a man who's not in love," Molly said thoughtfully.

"It's not love, it's a constitutional dislike of having his carefully laid plans thrown into disarray," Letty explained. "I imagine it's the businessman in him. He's accustomed to getting what he wants. And he doesn't always play by the rules."

"You're overlooking something here," Molly said. "If he still wants you after everything he's been through, he must see you as more than just a business acquisition. Seems to me you've done plenty of things in the past few days to make him think twice about your suitability as a wife."

"This time I've gone too far. After the way I abandoned him at that motel this morning, he's not going to want me any longer. He'll wash his hands of me and look elsewhere for a suitable wife. I just know it. I blew my last chance to make the relationship work." Letty sprinkled a few more peppers on her half of the pizza.

"Wait and see."

"No, it's over. Finished. I should have stayed there and talked instead of running off like that. But the truth is, I've had it with being made to look like a fool."

Molly made a face as she chewed pizza. "If it's any consolation, I'm not feeling like the sharpest brain on campus at the moment, either. Not after I realized how my own investigation had been monitored and sabotaged right from the start by that mysterious Hawk person."

Letty looked up. "Did he finally identify himself to you?"

"Uh-huh. I turned on the computer this morning and there was a message from him. The first one he's signed."

"What did it say?"

"It said 'see you at the wedding.' That was my first inkling that I'd been had." Molly finished the bite of pizza and reached for her wine. "I tell you, Letty, if I ever meet that jerk in person I'm going to have a few well-chosen words to say to him."

"Don't worry," Letty said. "You won't be seeing him at the wedding. There isn't going to be one." A shadow fell over the table and she glanced up quickly, hoping against hope. She stifled her disappointment when she saw Sheldon Peabody smiling genially.

He was wearing a pair of artfully faded jeans, a flower-print shirt unbuttoned halfway down his chest and several gold chains around his neck.

"Well, well, well. I believe this is where I came in." The gold chains glinted in the dim light as Sheldon sat down without waiting to be asked. "You two still have lousy taste in pizza, I see." He signaled for a beer.

"You don't have to eat any of it," Molly told him.

"Don't worry, I won't." Sheldon beamed at them as the beer was set down in front of him. "But to show you what a great sport I am, I'll pay for it."

Letty and Molly stared at him in shock.

Letty recovered first. "You'll pay for it? You're going to buy us dinner?"

"Are you feeling all right, Sheldon?" Molly asked.

"I have never felt better in my life," Sheldon declared. "I'm celebrating." He hoisted his glass of beer. "Join me in a salute to the dazzling new future that awaits yours truly."

"What dazzling new future?" Letty demanded.

"Does this have anything to do with the missing buttons on your shirt and all those gold chains?" Molly inquired.

"It does, indeed. I am going off to find my destiny in Lala Land, ladies. I am blowing this two-bit burg," Sheldon announced grandly. "I'm shaking the dust of Tipton Cove from my feet and heading for life in the fast-forward lane where I belong. You may congratulate me, my dears. I have been invited to accept a position on the history faculty of Rothwell College. Full professor with tenure."

Letty stared at him. "Do I detect the fine hand of Jennifer Thorne?"

"Ah, yes. Dear little Jennifer." Sheldon inclined his head in acknowledgment. "The lovely Ms. Thorne has decided I would make a great scholarly contribution to Rothwell and she prevailed upon her father to so inform the trustees of the college. Once Mr. Thorne let it be known that there would be no more Thorne endowments for the college unless they made the appointment, they fell all over themselves making me an offer I couldn't refuse."

Molly grinned slowly. "Congratulations, Sheldon. Something tells me you'll do very well down in Southern California."

"Listen," Sheldon leaned forward to announce with exuberant confidence, "I was born for Southern California."

Letty smiled. "Good luck, Sheldon," she said sincerely.

"Thank you, my dear. I want you to know you are at least partially responsible for my good fortune. Jennifer Thorne was quite taken with the way I decked Augustine at the banquet that first night. She says she's been looking for a man with real machismo."

"And since you're looking for a woman with connections, the match should be a perfect one," Molly murmured.

Sheldon chose to ignore that. "Speaking of our dear Saint Augustine, where is he?"

"Right here," Xavier said from directly behind him. "And I want everyone to know upfront that I am not feeling in a really saintly mood."

Letty jumped at the sound of his deep, rough voice. *"Xavier!"* She looked up at him with undisguised longing and was startled by what she saw.

Xavier needed a shave. He had always reminded her of a well-groomed gangster but tonight the dark shadow of a beard gave him an even more dangerous look. He was wearing the expensive trousers he'd had on this morning and one of his beautifully tailored white shirts. But both garments had dust and grease stains on them and they were distinctly rumpled. There were scuff marks on his handmade shoes. He looked like what Letty had briefly assumed him to be, a man with an unsavory past.

"How did you get back?" Molly asked with open curiosity.

"I hitched a ride with a trucker as far as Portland and then rented a car to drive over here to the coast. It's been a long trip, to put it mildly. I have suffered. Nothing but lousy truckstop coffee and greasy truckstop hamburgers for the entire trip."

"Oh, dear." Letty turned red. "I'm sorry, Xavier."

"You should be." He sat down.

"No offense, but you look like hell, Augustine." Sheldon smiled cheerfully.

"Peabody, if you have any sense at all, you will keep your mouth shut," Xavier told him.

Sheldon shrugged good-naturedly and leaned back in his chair to sip his beer.

Xavier turned to Letty who was toying with a slice of pizza. "Now that I've finally caught up with you at last, we are going to have a short talk."

He was going to say goodbye, once and for all. Letty just knew it. "Xavier, please, I know I shouldn't have run off like that this morning. I really am sorry. I realize you probably don't understand and it's hard to explain, but I—"

"Open your mouth, Letty," Xavier ordered calmly. He picked up a slice of pizza.

Letty's mouth dropped open more in surprise rather than in response to the command. "Huh?"

Xavier inserted the tip of the pizza wedge between her teeth. "Close your mouth."

Letty obeyed, bemused.

"Now, let's get one thing clear before we go through any more chase scenes," Xavier said. He folded his arms on the table and narrowed his eyes. "I love you."

Letty's eyes widened and she struggled to speak around the pizza. "Youff douff?" She chewed and swallowed hurriedly.

"Yes." Xavier inserted more pizza before she could finish the first bite, effectively silencing her again. "Nod your head if you still love me."

Letty nodded frantically.

"In spite of my past?"

Letty nodded again, wishing she had not put quite so many hot peppers on the pizza.

"What past is that?" Sheldon asked.

Xavier paid no heed to the question. His eyes were fixed on Letty's face. "I am sorry I didn't tell you everything right from the start. My only excuse is that I was afraid of losing you. You have my word there won't be any more secrets between us, ever. Good enough?"

"Yeff." Letty swallowed another bite of pizza. When Xavier made a commitment, you knew he'd stand by it. "Oh, yes, Xavier."

"Good. That's settled, then. On to other things. I want your solemn vow that you will never again abandon me in a cheap motel on the Interstate. That was an extremely tacky thing to do, Letty."

Still struggling with a mouthful of pizza, Letty started to nod and then shook her head quickly.

Xavier smiled a little dangerously. "Is that a yes or a no?"

Letty swallowed the pizza. "It's a yes. I mean a no. I mean I won't abandon you in any more cheap motels on the Interstate."

"This is beginning to sound more interesting by the minute," Molly observed. "Does that vow include not abandoning him in luxury resort hotels, too?"

Xavier again ignored the interruption, his entire attention on Letty who just stared back at him, knowing her heart was probably mirrored in her eyes.

"I think," Xavier said coolly, "that we have been through enough fun and games. I am now officially declaring this case of bridal jitters at an end."

"Oh, Xavier, are you sure?"

"I've been sure since the beginning." Xavier got to his feet. His mouth edged upward at the corner. "Come on, honey, we have things to do."

"Like what?" Letty got to her feet.

"Like addressing wedding invitations. But first things first." Xavier caught her around her hips and tossed her lightly over his shoulder.

"Xavier, for heaven's sake. Everyone's watching," Letty gasped, torn between giggles and outrage.

Xavier glanced at a grinning Molly. "By the way, Molly, Hawk says to send his regards and to tell you he intends to go hunting soon."

Molly's grin turned instantly into a thunderous scowl. "I do not approve of hunting wild animals."

"I don't think wild animals are the quarry Hawk has in mind," Xavier said. "Good night, Molly. So long, Peabody. I hear you're going to Southern California. Something tells me you'll like it down there."

"Bound to be a lot more exciting than Tipton Cove," Sheldon agreed.

"I wouldn't be too sure about that," Xavier said. He swung around and strode through the crowded restaurant with Letty over his shoulder. A cheer went up as the diners realized what was happening.

"Hey, look," a young woman sitting at a nearby table remarked to her companion as Letty was carried past. "Isn't that Professor Conroy?"

"Yeah," her friend said in obvious amazement. "It is. Who would have thought she was the type to get herself carried off over a man's shoulder? Saint Augustine's shoulder, no less."

"He doesn't look too saintly right now," the young woman observed. "In fact, he looks kind of exciting."

"You know," Letty said to Xavier as she craned her head to wave farewell to Molly, "things like this never used to happen to the old Letty Conroy."

Xavier laughed as he carried her outside to the waiting Jaguar. The sound echoed through the night, deep and rich and full of male happiness.

A LONG TIME LATER, Letty stirred amid the tangled sheets of her bed and stroked her fingertips along Xavier's smoothly muscled shoulder.

"When did you know for certain that you loved me?" she asked.

"I knew you were just biding your time until you asked that question. Couldn't resist, could you?" Xavier propped himself up on one elbow and looked down at her. His green eyes gleamed in the shadows.

"Well, you didn't love me at first," she insisted.

"What makes you so sure of that?" He put his hand on her hip.

"The fact that you had me investigated. The fact that you didn't try to make love to me for a long while." Letty started counting on her fingers. "The fact that you originally selected me for the great honor of being your bride based on my dull past and equally uneventful present. Shall I go on?"

"No." He snagged her fingers and trapped them on the bed. Then he studied her thoughtfully for a long moment. "You're wrong, you know."

She smiled gently. "It's all right, Xavier. You don't have to pretend it was love at first sight the way it was on my part. As long as you're sure you love me now, I don't care."

"I think it was love at first sight." He smiled at her skeptical expression. "It's true, Letty. I'll admit I didn't label it love in the beginning. To be bluntly honest about it, I wasn't thinking in those terms. I was just keeping an eye out for the woman who met all my specifications. The minute I was introduced to you, I knew you were the one."

Letty gave a choked laugh. "So I met your specifications and you noticed right off? That's not what I'd call falling in love at first sight. You chose your bride the same way you would have if you'd been living in medieval times and you know it. You wanted a suitable wife."

"I found her. And then she made me woo and win her. Which she had every right to do." Xavier drew her fingers to his lips and kissed them warmly. "I found myself chasing after her, doing battle with rivals for her hand and rescuing her. Then it began to dawn on me that what I was feeling might be what people call love. I knew it for certain when you decided to save me from my past."

"Really?" Letty glowed.

"Really." Xavier's eyes were very intent now. "No one's ever tried to rescue me before, Letty."

"I felt like such a fool when I realized it was all a game," she confided.

"It wasn't a game. Not the way you mean. I was indulging myself in the luxury of knowing you cared that much." He kissed her fingers again. "It was very reassuring. Men like a little assurance, too, you know. Forgive me?"

"Yes." She was feeling wonderfully magnanimous at the moment. "Especially since I've decided that the investigation you had your friend Hawk carry out was a good thing in the end. After all, if it hadn't been for that, I might still be leading the same uneventful life I've been leading for the past twenty-nine years. As it is, I'm a whole new person. I owe it all to you."

Xavier groaned. "At the risk of repeating myself, I would just like to point out one more time that I was perfectly content with the old you."

"Don't be silly. I'm sure I'm a lot more interesting these days." Letty kissed him lingeringly on the mouth.

"That's not what I was thinking when I found myself hitchhiking a ride out on the Interstate." Xavier cupped her breast in his hand.

"No? What were you thinking?" She kissed his throat.

"I was thinking that I should have fulfilled your craving for a taste of the wild side a lot earlier in our relationship by taking you to bed. I think if I'd done that, I could have saved myself a lot of exhausting effort."

"But you're so good at chasing around after me," she murmured.

"Making love to you is a lot more interesting." Xavier eased her onto her back and came down on top of her. "Something tells me I am never going to get tired of it."

"What about the rest of those wedding invitations we're supposed to be addressing?"

"First thing in the morning," he vowed. Then he clasped her wrists in his hands and moved them up above her head, stretching her out beneath him. His mouth closed over hers, hot, possessive and loving.

Letty felt her whole body quicken once more beneath his touch. "I love you, Xavier," she whispered.

"I love you, too. And the next time you want proof, just ask, okay?"

"I'll do that," she said with a soft smile.

But there was no need for proof. Their love glowed between them, clear and bright and strong enough to last a lifetime.

TOO WILD TO WED? by Jayne Ann Krentz

Xavier Augustine had had his fiancée investigated to find out if she were perfect wife material. Letty Conroy had led a scandal-free life, but she determined that this impudent man would find something wild and naughty about her . . .

TERMINALLY SINGLE by Kate Jenkins

Family tradition dictated that Ashley Atwood would be the next maiden aunt, and no man had ever tempted her to fight her fate. Then sexy Michael Jordan crossed her path and set about finding the fire which lurked beneath her button-tight exterior.

A MAN FOR THE NIGHT by Maggie Baker

Lust – not love – turned Susan Harkness into the passionate woman who had dragged Nick Taurage to bed on their first – and only – date. She had wanted to impress her colleagues and Nick was the most intriguing man she had ever met, but he was *not* the man for her.

THAT STUBBORN YANKEE by Carla Neggers

Harlan Rockwood's ex-wife was a woman to be approached with caution. Hot-tempered, dangerously beautiful, Beth had already once ordered him out of her life. He couldn't decide whether the thugs who were out to get him or hiding out with Beth would be the more hazardous to his health.

Spoil yourself next month
with these four novels from

— TEMPTATION —

TANGLED LIVES by JoAnn Ross
(sequel to TANGLED HEARTS)

Reporter Mitch Cantrell wasn't about to let the sexy and provocative singer, La Rubia, seduce General Ramirez. Behind the green contact lenses and clinging dresses, was a woman Mitch recognised. They had once shared a dangerous assignment and nights of passion – and he refused to let another man have her.

THE LAST GREAT AFFAIR by Kristine Rolofson

Arianna Simone couldn't believe her bad luck. First, she went to the *wrong* wedding. Then, she was kidnapped by the best man, who believed she was a femme fatale out to ruin the nuptials!

BEN & LIZ & TONI & ROSS by Frances Davies

Tall, dark and handsome – I'd been waiting all my life for a man like Ben Malloy. Only Toni, my roommate and best friend, hadn't. She and I were like sisters – always looking out for each other. Now that I'd found my own hero, I had a choice to make: exclusive friendship, or exclusive love.

LOVE COUNTS by Karen Percy

The cards told Lindsay that she was destined to meet Mr. Right. But they neglected to mention that he would be the wrong Mr. Right. Tim Reynolds – her hunky business partner and a *younger* man.

4

Temptations and 2 gifts yours FREE!

Here's an invitation for you to treat yourself for FREE to all that's most daring and provocative in modern love stories, with 4 Temptations, a CUDDLY TEDDY and a special MYSTERY GIFT.

And, if you choose, go on to enjoy 4 exciting Temptations, each month delivered direct to your door for just £1.65 each. Send the coupon below to: **Reader Service, FREEPOST, PO Box 236, Croydon, Surrey CR9 9EL.**

- - - - - - - - - - - - - `NO STAMP REQUIRED` - - - - - - - - - - - - -

Yes! Please rush me my 4 free Temptations and 2 free gifts! Please also reserve me a Reader Service subscription. If I decide to subscribe I can look forward to receiving 4 Temptations each month for just £6.60 delivered direct to my door, postage and packing free, plus a free monthly newsletter. If I choose not to subscribe I shall write to you within 10 days - I can keep the books and gifts whatever I decide. I may cancel or suspend my subscription at any time. I am over 18 years of age.

Name Mrs/Miss/Ms/Mr———————————————— EP15T

Address ————————————————————

————————————————————————

Postcode ———————— Signature ————————